SPLINTERED

By David Perkins

Introduction:

You are about to experience an adventure. Whether you take this adventure in a lounge chair by the beach or pool, in a doctor's office, possibly an easy chair, or after going to bed, SPLINTERED is an adventure that you will not want to put down. We all have our ups and downs, our triumphs and our tragedies. We live in a world of political turmoil and strife, a world filled with problems that we desperately seek an escape from, if only briefly. The problems we face daily may not be the same as our neighbors but we all have problems. SPLINTERED is the story of the Whitman's, a fictional family, but a family like ours that faces tough struggles each and every day. If you struggle with problems, worries, or concerns then this book is for you. We all have our own battles to fight but we do not have to fight them alone.

Mr. Perkins takes the reader from the deepest, darkest valley to the highest pinnacle of a mountain top in SPLINTERED. There will be sudden drops and loops that will turn your world upside down. There are vivid word pictures and even stories within the story that draw you in and make you feel that you are there witnessing the events as they unfold. If a quest for adventure burns within you then SPLINTERED is a must read for you. "Enjoy the ride!"

SPLINTERED

By David Perkins

Edited by Becky Burkhalter (1998)

David Perkins (2019)

This work was originally entitled, *Hey, James Is My Brother!* and self-published in 1998. This work has been rewritten and is now entitled, *SPLINTERED*.

© Copy 2019 by David Perkins

Dedication

This book is dedicated primarily to my parents, Coy and Tera Perkins. It was their unfailing love, teaching, and daily example that taught me the values to live by. Growing up in the turbulent sixties was difficult, but was made easier by the firm foundation, love, and Faith that we shared in our home.

Additionally, this book is dedicated to my wife and children for their patience and assistance while this work was in progress. Since the original writing of this book, previously entitled **_Hey, James Is My Brother!_**, I have been blessed with three wonderful grandchildren Rayleigh, Raylan, and Emeline as well as our "Little Jessie" who is awaiting us in Heaven. I would feel remiss if I left them out as they are such an important part of my life and make my life complete.

Lastly, this book is dedicated to all my friends, former students, and to you the reader. May God bless you and may this book give you the courage and endurance to face your daily struggles and problems no matter how

insurmountable they may appear, even when your life is **_SPLINTERED._**

REVIEWS

__Splintered__ is a masterful story told through the compassionate fingertips of a writer who cares for the very soul of his reader. The poetic word paintings are easily absorbed through the mind's eye of even a casual reader while the stark realism of tragedy quickens the deep emotions of even the apathetic. Thanks, David, for taking the time and effort to share your heart.

Steve C. Jarvis

As I read *__Splintered__*, I was very touched with the feelings and understanding that David was able to put into words for those who live daily with a physical handicap. Thanks, David, for a wonderful story!

Lyndal Tatum

I picked up *__Splintered__* late one night and began reading before bed. I didn't put it down again until I finished several hours later.

Cindy Waters Woodcock

SPLINTERED

CHAPTER I

T hick, acrid smoke slowly filled the car and a deathly stillness gripped the darkened forest. The only sound that pierced the silence was the soft trickle of the small, rocky stream nearby. The car lay on its side dying, belching its venomous breath as one last tire slowed its rotation and then silently, stopped. Somewhere in its bowels a mixture of anti-freeze, gasoline, and oil began to drip onto its dead but still warm heart. Gin awoke to a feeling of pain and bewilderment not remembering where she was or how she got there. As soon as she was born, her father saw her beautiful auburn hair and then and there decided to call her Ginger. For convenience, it was later shortened to Gin. She was also known for having a quick temper to match her auburn hair.

Slowly she began to put the pieces together. She remembered a party, James's party. James was Gin's younger brother who had turned thirteen today. Now she remembered; it was James' "coming out" party as mom and dad called it. Her mind drifted back to her "coming out" party two years ago when she had become a teenager. She remembered dining in the fancy restaurant all dressed up with her mom and dad. "Mom and Dad!" she yelled out, "where's mom and dad?"

There were shapes all around her, but it was so dark and smoky; Gin could not make any of them out. Just then she heard a low grunting noise that sounded "animal like," but she realized that it came from inside the car and not outside. "Dad, dad!" she yelled as one of the shapes in front of her began to move.

Gin tried to reach her dad, but she couldn't move. No matter how she twisted or turned, she was trapped. Finally, she realized that something was holding her; it was pinning her down. What ever it was, it was soft and warm, and it smelled, but the smell was a nice smell. It was a familiar smell that made her think of love and home. She wanted to get closer to it, to wrap herself up in it and just go to sleep. But there was something haunting about it too. She had smelled it so many times before. It was her mother's perfume! "Mom, mom" she screamed! No matter how much she coaxed, shook, or cried, her mother would not move or make a sound. Her clothes felt all wet and sticky, and Gin knew that she had to be hurt badly, real badly.

Gin knew that it was up to her to get help, and she had to get it fast. Slowly she began working her legs out from under her mom. With her legs free she tried again to move, but she was still held fast. It was almost as if she were glued to the seat.

11

Gin racked her brain for a solution. "My seatbelt! I must be losing my mind" Gin thought.

Gin was the only member of her family who ever wore a seatbelt. Everyone else said they were too uncomfortable. Carefully she worked her hands under her mom and located the square, silver buckle on the belt. Pressing the little star in the middle set her free. Gravity took over, and Gin slid sideways across the back seat. For the first time she drew in a deep breath and choked on the stale air.

Coughing and gagging, Gin felt her way and crawled over to her father. "Dad, dad!" she cried, "mom's hurt." He was conscious now but when he spoke it was garbled and made no sense. Deliriously he began talking about the party and the birthday cake with thirteen candles. Gin was in trouble and she knew it. "Don't panic," she thought. "Get control of yourself. Think first, then act, just like dad taught you."

She had to get help for her mom and dad. It was so dark she couldn't even make out where James was. "Dad, listen to me," she said. "I'm going for help. Just lay still and rest, I'll be right back." Little did she know that hours would pass before she saw them again.

The car had landed on its side and after skidding down the hillside had come to rest against an ancient oak tree. The tree had monstrous arms that appeared to sweep down as if to hold them prisoner. Its deep, furrowed bark echoed the centuries of history it had witnessed. Thick gray Spanish moss adorned the fingers on the tree branches and wafted in the gentle breeze. Yet, in the darkness, its long, spiraled, gray locks gave it an evil and sinister appearance.

Since the car was laying on its side, Gin couldn't open the doors next to the ground. She tried the other doors above her but either they were stuck or she didn't have the strength to push them open. Again, she felt helpless, trapped. For a moment she was a caged animal. Frantically she scurried about the car beating on windows and kicking doors. Breathless and choking she settled down and tried to pull herself back together.

"Think," she said to herself. Lost in the darkness, she slowly and meticulously began working her fingers around all the windows and doors. Suddenly, something gave way and collapsed. Losing her balance, Gin fell forward as jagged glass sliced open her arm. Instinct told her to jerk her arm back, but she was in control now. She knew if she pulled back she could cut her arm even more as she pulled it back through the glass. Carefully she felt around her and found something made of cloth, probably one of James' presents. "Where is James?" she thought. She held the cloth in her left hand

and flipped it over and over until her hand was well wrapped. She began to push on the glass, but there was very little to push.

"Lucky her," she thought, she had found the one place where glass was left and from the stinging she felt, she believed she had managed to shred her arm. She took the rag, cleared the jagged edges away, and put her arm through. As she pushed her head through, the fresh air hit her like smelling salts. Wide awake now, Gin pulled and squirmed until she worked her way through the shattered window.

Almost the entire rear window was gone. Gin struggled to her feet and let the fresh air bathe her and cleanse her lungs. The fresh air also brought back the reality of the situation along with her mission. She knew they wouldn't be found this deep in the woods. Unless, unless someone happened to see the wreck. She paused and listened; again, the only sound was the melodic trickle of running water from somewhere nearby. No one was coming, and she knew it.

Gin knew the only help she could expect was from the highway. But where was it? It was so dark and there was no moon out tonight. "Oh God!" she cried. "Please help me. Somebody, please help me!" She began to sob quietly at first, but the tears grew as the minutes passed slowly in the great forest of her fears. Her tears would have fallen on deaf ears and faded into the blackness except for one that listened far, far away, yet, was also right beside her.

Frank didn't know why he and Ruth had left so early that night for the movie. For some reason they were way ahead of schedule. Ruth suggested they take advantage of the situation and take the long way to town. She thought it would be nice not to be in a hurry for a change. The long leisurely back road to town would be a pleasant drive. Hardly anyone traveled on it anymore, and they could take their time and enjoy the cool night air.

Frank rolled the electric windows down on his new 1985 Eldorado and let the spring perfumes fill the car as they cruised down the old, winding highway. Ruth felt like a giddy teenager again out on her first date. Their children were grown now and had left the nest. Everything seemed to be falling into place for them. Frank had gotten the big promotion at work; they had paid off their house a year ago, and Frank was due to retire in little over a year. "Yes, everything is well with the world," Ruth thought, as she drank in the aroma of the new leather seats and the wild honeysuckle as they passed into the dark forest. Ruth was sitting back with her eyes closed and a little smile on her face when Frank shouted, "Look at that!"

"What's the matter," said Ruth looking a little startled.

"It's those kids again. They've been out here switching road signs again."

About twice a year for the past two years, some of the local teenagers had been pulling not only cruel but also dangerous pranks.

They would take signs from one road and switch them with signs on another road. Sometimes they would switch a right curve sign with a left curve sign or a twenty-five-mph sign with a fifty-five-mph sign. Often, they would remove a stop sign completely. On this particular night they had celebrated by switching curve signs.

Earlier, Gin's dad, deciding to take the unfamiliar route home and following the same deceptive signs, began making a left turn when he suddenly found himself traveling at sixty-five mph with a sharp turn to the right. Tires squealed, and everyone screamed, but there was no regaining control as the car careened sideways off the embankment becoming air-borne. The car landed on its side with an earth-shattering crash and skidded down the embankment. Upon impact a shower of glass diamonds filled the dark night air as the rear window exploded.

For a few brief moments the forest was filled with excitement and disorder. Awakened from their peaceful slumber, the day birds screeched and fluttered in the trees overhead. Bushes rattled and quivered as small animals raced away for their lives. Somewhere in the distance a raccoon chattered angrily. Then, once again, all was quiet and peaceful. The only evidence of the tragedy, of the lives that had been changed forever, was a few crushed wild shrubs and the sprinkle of glass that carpeted the forest floor. The car, along with all of its unintentional pilgrims, was swallowed into the depths of the darkened forest.

Unlike Jim, Frank and Ruth were familiar with the local delinquents' tricks and were always wary of the signs. Being a conscientious citizen, Frank told Ruth that they would call the police as soon as they got to the theater. Ruth eased back into her seat and returned to her utopia. In the blackness, they took no notice of the bruised and torn bushes as they neared the scene of the accident.

Gin had been waiting for what seemed an eternity in the cool, dark woods. Actually, she had been waiting only a few minutes. The living forest was now beginning to return to life since the deafening crash had driven the peace away. The night animals who had been silenced by the deafening crash now began to accept the alien form which had become a part of their world. Owls hooted, frogs croaked along the stream, and other strange creatures pierced the serenity of the forest with their mournful cries.

It was at that moment that Gin heard another

sound. The sound was a motor, somewhere off in the distance.

The highway, it had to be the highway. Now Gin knew which way to go. Focusing on the sound, she ran through trees fighting tree limbs and tripping over roots and logs on the ground. Over and over she fell and got up again until she finally reached the base of the embankment. Vines and briers grabbed her clothes and tried to tangle her feet as she clawed and fought her way to the top of the hill. The forest tried its best to hold its prisoner, but she was determined. She would not allow herself to be beaten. Bleeding and breathless, Gin finally reached the top of the summit. At the exact same moment, Frank and Ruth drove around the corner that had been a death trap for Gin and her family. Just as the car lights sliced through the misty blackness, Gin stepped onto the edge of the road. Ruth yelled, "Look out Frank!" He swerved just in time to miss Gin's stumbling figure coming out of the inky darkness. As he started to apply the brakes, Ruth shouted again, "What are you doing? Are you crazy?"

"She looked hurt," said Frank! "She might need some help."

"Think about it, Frank, did you see a car? What would she be doing out here in the middle of nowhere? She's probably one of those kids who changed the signs. You go back, and you'll probably get robbed or beaten or maybe even worse. You just drive on, we'll tell the police about her too. She's not our problem. Besides, did you see how messy she looked? Do you want her in our new car? No way!"

Reluctantly, Frank eased his foot back on the accelerator and began to apply pressure. His head said he was right, but his heart was breaking as he watched the figure in his rear-view mirror begin to fade and then to disappear.

Gin watched as the car slowed, stopped momentarily, and then sped off into the darkness. She watched in disbelief as the tail-lights grew smaller and smaller until they were just two red embers in the distance, and then they were gone. "Maybe they didn't see me," Gin thought, even though she knew better. "Surely someone else will come soon."

Seconds passed, then minutes. Finally, in the distance, Gin heard the faint roar of another motor. As the sound grew closer, Gin began to edge her way farther out onto the highway. When the lights came around the corner, Gin stepped into the middle of the highway and frantically began waving her arms.

Wayne Brantley was tired, sleepy, and basically angry at the world. He had worked the last town for two days and only sold ten Bibles. Only two of those were the deluxe gold-leaf edition which he made his largest commissions on. His sales would not even pay for his meals, let alone a motel room. And what did he find in those motel rooms but a Bible placed there for free by the Gideons. He couldn't win. It looked like he would be spending another night in the car.

Why did he ever start selling Bibles anyway? He was terrible at it. It seemed that all the other salesmen did better than he did. Why, for some reason even the salesmen that occasionally gave a Bible away to a widow did better than he did. Maybe it was his approach. He tried to seem sincere when he told people how badly they needed a Bible. However, almost without exception, it was always the same story. The wife would point at two or three Bibles on a shelf or coffee table and say they had enough Bibles and didn't need another one. As the door slowly closed in his face, the couple often mumbled that they didn't even have enough time to read the ones that they had. Why buy more?

It was also usually obvious that there was no use in returning because the Bibles they had were in mint condition and would not be wearing out anytime soon. Not in his lifetime anyway. That was exactly the kind of day that Wayne had suffered through today.

Now he was tired and wanted a drink and a soft

bed more than anything. He would not let anything or anyone keep him from reaching his goal. As he rounded a sharp corner, he saw something or someone ahead of him in the road. It was someone waving her arms and obviously wanting him to stop.

He could tell from a distance that it was a girl because of her long hair. As his Nissan Stanza slowed, he could see that her hair was matted and her face looked dirty-or, or was it bloody? He slowed to a crawl and then saw her real condition. Gunning the accelerator, he screeched off in a cloud of dust and gravel and then disappeared into the night.

Gin was about to ask for his help, but she didn't have the opportunity. Before she could open her mouth, Wayne looked into her swollen eyes and battered face and then suddenly, he was gone. For a split second, Gin was able to recognize a look of pity in his eyes and a stack of leather-bound Bibles beside him on the seat. Once again, the last sight she saw of him was his taillights as the car screamed away. Gin forgot many things about the accident but the look on Wayne's face and the Bibles on the seat were seared into her memory forever.

As Wayne drove through the night, he thought to himself, "Probably a boyfriend-girlfriend thing. He'll probably come back and pick her up anyway.

I can't get involved in that. I'd probably have to go to the police station and fill out papers. I might even get sued. No sir, not me! She got herself into this mess; let her get herself out." "I know," he thought, easing his conscience. "I'll call the police and tell them. I can just hang up and not tell them who I am or anything. I'll be in the clear. Let the police deal with it."

Sometime later, after his third drink, Wayne thought, "I know there was something I was supposed to do. Oh well, maybe I'll think of it later," he said. "It must not have been too important. If somebody needed a Bible, he can call back or he can just forget about it. It's his problem, not mine." Turning the glass slowly, Wayne noticed the pretty amber color of the liquid inside when he held it up to the light. Noticing a dirty spot on the edge of the glass, he rotated it to a cleaner side and then downed the stinging venom.

This time Gin's heart was broken; her knees buckled, and she sank collapsing down onto the asphalt and gravel and wept uncontrollably. "God, I need you. I can't do this alone."

Suddenly her hands became visible and began to take shape on the pavement. Then, ever so slowly, she began to see colors as her tattered dress became illuminated. Looking behind her, she could see her shadow begin to take shape and focus its distinct outlines on the pavement. Her shadow danced from side to side as the lights approached unsteadily. There was a car or something coming toward her. Gin's auburn hair began to glow in the darkness as the lights came closer and closer.

The vehicle, whatever it was, sure was noisy. Suddenly Gin panicked as she realized that she was sitting right in the middle of the road. The lights grew brighter and brighter as the vehicle closed the distance between them. Looking through her tears, the lights blurred and little orbs swirled in her watering eyes as she tried her best to look into the approaching headlights to determine if it was a friend or a foe. By just sitting there, was she once again staring death in the face? This time there was no seatbelt to protect her from what was coming directly at her.

Frantically she began to flop around like a fish out of water. It was useless. No matter how hard she tried, she couldn't stand or crawl out of the way. Once again, with all of her strength gone; she collapsed to the pavement. Trembling, Gin turned her face away and clinching her eyes and teeth, braced for the impact that would end her life.

The vehicle slowed as it neared the crumpled and broken figure on the pavement. It's worn brakes screeched, and the old hull of a muffler rumbled as the old truck rolled to a stop. Gin remembered a door slamming and feet running toward her as her brain slipped into neutral and everything began fading away.

The last thing she heard were the words, "I've got you sweetheart, I've got you." They were soft words; words of comfort and of love. Gin knew she was safe in the arms that cradled her. She knew there was nothing to fear. Though they had never met, Gin felt shielded, protected from any and all danger. Relinquishing what little will she had left, Gin passed out.

CHAPTER II

G abe Michaels and his two grandchildren, Will and Kelli, had spent a leisurely day fishing together on a nearby lake. These days, he liked to spend as much time as possible with them. Gabe looked at the world differently than he did just two months ago. His doctors had told him two months ago that he had an inoperable brain tumor and that for the time being, he could lead a normal life-style. They also reported that he would suffer a loss of memory and severe paralysis before his death. Because of this demon that haunted him, he lived every day as if it were his last. "One day there may be a cure," Gabe thought. "This is 1985 and miracles do still happen." But Gabe refused to be afraid. He had been very afraid as he stormed the beaches of Normandy on June 6, 1944. The fear of death had brought him closer to God. Now he knew that he never had to fear, as he had so many years ago as he lay on that bloody, sandy beach at Normandy. Now Gabe watched every sunrise and relished every sunset. Each breath was honeyed with aromas, and he drank them in as if they were a dessert.

The doctors told him that his tumor was a

slow-growing kind and that he could expect to live for two or, if he were lucky, maybe two and a half years. Gabe had always been a kind, caring person. His friends, which were many, knew him best by his motto, "There aren't any strangers in this world, only friends that I've never met." Although Gabe had always put others ahead of himself, now he was especially sensitive to the needs of others. The eyes through which Gabe saw the world, although still as blue as the sky, now saw every flower and every bird singing in a tree and danced with glee as his grandchildren giggled and played.

It was these caring blue eyes that first spotted the crumpled figure on the road. As the old truck screeched to a halt, the old man leaped from the worn seat and ran to the young girl as she crumpled to the pavement. He was just in time to wrap his big arms around her before her head collided with the asphalt.

Looking around, Gabe saw no one else, no car, nothing. He knew she needed help, and she had to have it fast. Cradling her in his arms as he would a baby fawn, he lifted her gently and carried her to the pick-up. His two grandchildren, alert to the situation, had already begun to toss excess baggage into the back of the truck. Drink cans, life jackets, Gabe's hat which had fallen off when he raced from the truck, and all other kinds of paraphernalia zoomed out of the cab of the old truck. Some were even fortunate enough to land in the back of the truck; others just disappeared into the night.

Kelli and Will helped Gabe slide Gin onto the truck seat. They sat on each side of her in order to brace her and to keep her from falling. When they first saw her condition, they were taken aback but immediately constrained themselves and did what had to be done. Will let Gin's head rest on his shoulder and Kelli helped keep it stationary. Gabe dropped the truck into gear and the engine roared to life, life that it had not experienced in years.

"Hang tough old girl, you can do it," Gabe said as the speedometer passed eighty.

Gin drifted in and out of consciousness on the way to the hospital. Later she remembered the lines on the road blending together and the telephone poles looking only inches apart as the old truck flew down the highway. Finally, she allowed her rigid body to relax, and she drifted off into a world where there were no problems, no accidents, and no pain.

Abruptly her peaceful world was shattered by an intense pain that seemed to pierce her very soul. She tried to blink but her eyes were held firmly open by the doctor's skillful hands. The light was so bright and painful that tears began to flow once again from her eyes.

"No apparent brain damage; her pupils are reacting normally," stated the doctor.

"How did the x-rays turn out?" asked Dr. Samuelson.

"All appear normal except for her right index finger. There appears to be a small fracture, but other than that she appears to be ok."

"I'll want to review those x-rays again as soon as we are sure that she is stable. She does have some internal bruising but nothing to be overly concerned about. Let's go ahead and splint that finger and get her cleaned up a bit. Has anyone contacted the police or her family?"

"The police are in the waiting room with the man that brought her in. She didn't have any identification on her, so we don't know whom to contact."

"Let me know as soon as she regains consciousness and we'll see if we can find out something about her family. Unless her condition worsens, we will keep her a couple of days for observation and then release her if she---"

The doctor never finished his sentence. Gin sat straight up and began screaming and thrashing with her arms. The battle was short lived as everyone ran to her aid. Soon afterward she was lying still and sobbing quietly.

Gently the doctor took her hand and said, "It's

okay, just settle down a little. You're safe now. Can you tell me what your name is?"

Seconds passed but finally her lips began to move, and softly, "Gin," was released from her lips.

"Gin, I need to ask you some questions; do you think you can answer them?" Gin lay motionless, her eyes darting from side to side. Slowly she focused on the doctor and nodded.

"Gin, you're in the hospital. Mostly you are just scratched and bruised." The doctor cut his eyes toward a nurse. "Get the officer please." The nurse stepped to the door and motioned for the officer to come in. He paused just inside the door and removed a pad and pen from his pocket.

Dr. Samuelson began again, "Gin can you tell me what happened to you?"

"Uh," she hesitated, "I think I, I mean there was an, Mama, where's my mama and daddy," she screamed at the top of her lungs.

Again, she sat up and began thrashing around, and again the doctor and nurse had to settle her down. "Are my mom and dad ok?" she asked.

Dr. Samuelson didn't know what to say; for a moment he was speechless. "First things first, young lady."

"Are my mom and dad dead?" Gin whimpered.

"Well to be perfectly honest, I don't know Gin.

You're going to have to help me find out."

"You mean they aren't here?" Gin asked.

"No, Gin, they're not. Tell me what happened."

"We were going home from uh, an um."

"It's all right, Gin, take your time," the doctor said.

Gin's eyes grew wider and began to dart rapidly from side to side again as memories began to float to the surface. Then she began to tremble and shake.

"What is it, Gin; you can tell me?"

"An accident, a wreck, we, dad tried to stop. The car just started sliding sideways, I saw trees coming at me. Then we rolled over and over. I had to climb a hill to get out. Nobody would help me! "

"Gin, listen to me, listen." The doctor cupped Gin's face in his soft hands and turned her face where he could look directly into her eyes. Gin, you mentioned your mom and dad; were they with you?"

"Yes, they were, where are they?" Gin responded.

Dr. Samuelson and the nurse turned toward the officer who had paused taking notes. No words were exchanged, but the officer got the message.

The officer stuck his head out the door and

asked if Gabe was still there. Quietly Gabe slipped into the room as if it were holy ground. Slipping into the shadows, Gabe removed his hat and nervously began to roll it around and around through his two hands.

"Lay back and relax now Gin," said the doctor.

The officer turned toward Gabe, but Gabe's eyes were locked on the fragile figure lying just feet away on the table. His tousled, thinning gray locks were quite disheveled with many points on his head which in appearance resembled the points on a crown.

"Is she going to be ok?" whispered Gabe."

"Yes, she should be fine," the doctor whispered back. "But we have another problem, and we may need you to help again."

"Sure," said Gabe. " 'Whatcha' need?"

"Gabe, this is Gin, and she says that she was in an automobile accident. Did you see any sign of an accident?"

Gabe put his hand on the two-day growth of gray stubble on his chin and faded into deep thought. As he rubbed his chin, he began shaking his head. "No, I didn't see anything out of the ordinary. But then again, I was watching her; she was in the middle of the road, and I knew she needed help. I could have missed something very easily but I didn't see anyone else or a car or anything."

All this time Gin was playing the accident over and over in her mind as she lay on the table. They had wrapped her in warm blankets but even then, you could still see her shaking. Abruptly Gin yelled, "James!" startling the other four people in the room.

"What is it, Gin?"

"I remember, we had been to James's birthday party. Is James here? Where is everybody?"

"Gin, we don't know yet, but I can promise you we will find them. Was there anyone else in the car?"

Gin thought for a moment, "No, no, it was just the four of us."

The officer turned to Gabe, "Gabe, are you up to another ride in the country? It looks like somebody else needs your help."

Gabe was already half-way to the door. "If you're a 'comin' with me, you'd better come on. Otherwise, I'll be a 'drivin' that black and white and 'runnin' them sirens all by myself." By this time Gabe's grandchildren had been retrieved by their parents and Gabe was free to act.

Within eight minutes the police, with Gabe leading the charge, followed by two ambulances, were back where Gabe had found Gin.

There was little light out, and it looked somewhat like an alien movie out on the dark highway. There were flashlights everywhere, dancing on the road, hopping along the tree tops, and piercing the rough brush on the sides of the road. After several minutes one of the officers yelled, "Over here!" As everyone rushed toward the officer, Gabe reflected later that the scene looked like the attack of the giant fireflies.

On the road were two distinct, long skid marks. At first, they were unmistakably clear with distinct, crisp edges. All the rescuers followed the trail with all their lights trained on the two skid marks. They all took short little steps and appeared to move as one. Each group followed a separate skid mark, now Gabe thought the officers resembled a pair of alien millipedes from outer space with great glowing moving legs.

Then the skid marks began to become fuzzier and less distinct. Suddenly they began to grow markedly wider.

"What happened here?" one of the volunteers questioned.

One of the officers spoke up, "At first he was skidding forward, but it was too late. When he tried to regain control, the car began sliding sideways; that's why the marks are wider.

They followed the marks until the asphalt disappeared and the dirt began. The grass was really torn up, and the bushes on the side of the road were demolished. All at once the volunteers caught the scent of the trail and were off like hounds on the chase.

The car was not hard to find. There was a pretty clear path all the way down to the wounded automobile. Inside the car were Fran and Jim Whitman, Gin's parents. At first it was hard to tell if they were still alive or not. When the lights were first shone on them, they had a death-like pale appearance. They were both motionless and there was dried blood all over them. This could be either good or bad news. It was good if their bleeding had stopped and they were just unconscious. However, it could also mean that their hearts were still and were no longer pumping blood.

As the rescuers scanned the scene with their flashlights, one of the lights happened to cross Jim Whitman's face. An arm suddenly flew through the air, as a reflex, Jim had struggled to shield his face from the blinding light. The startled rescuers began whooping and hollering.

"Get a stretcher down here; we've got a live one!" one of the men shouted.

Not one but two very alive people were pulled from the wreckage that night. Both had multiple injuries, which required immediate treatment. Jim had a broken ankle, several broken ribs, and a multitude of cuts and bruises from tumbling down the embankment. Fran wasn't as fortunate. She had severe lacerations on her arms and face. The worse news was that she had multiple internal injuries which had caused internal bleeding and would require immediate surgery. She had gray, ashen color skin, and her abdomen was hard with all the blood that had pooled there from the internal bleeding. Within ten minutes both were on their way to the hospital. Jim was rapidly stabilizing while Fran was gradually slipping away.

As the sirens began to yell their call of distress and their flashing lights began fading into the night, the rescuers turned and headed back down the hill.

Joe, one of the investigating officers was getting ready to secure the scene.

"Wait a minute there, Joe," said the officer in charge. The officer was reading something he had picked up in the debris. "We may just have another victim. The girl in the hospital said that she had a brother in the car too."

"Captain, are you sure he wasn't traveling in another car or with someone else?"

"Positive. I was told that he was a younger brother."

"Well, this here's a birthday card that says,

"Happy Birthday James."

"He must be here somewhere. I just got so caught up when we found the parents you know. Well you know how it is."

"Pull that seat over and see if he is under it." For several minutes they tugged and pulled until they bent the seat enough to get a light under it. But there wasn't anyone to be found.

"Hey, you guys get back over here! It doesn't look like this search is over yet."

When the officer made his call for assistance, Gabe came skidding back down the hill.

"The girl at the hospital said something about a brother and about going to a party tonight. Look around and see if you can find any sign of him," said officer Johnson, who was in charge. Meanwhile he manned the radio and began the process of renewing the search.

The officer on duty at the station agreed to check other hospitals in the area to see if James had shown up there. After all, it had been almost three hours since the accident; he may have walked away just like his sister. The officer radioed back in less than two minutes that no thirteen-year old boys had been admitted to any hospitals in the area in the last twelve hours. All the searchers were beginning to filter out of the woods and gather back around the car. "Nothing," was all that each one of them said.

Inspector Johnson was baffled, "Could he have gone for help or could he be seriously hurt and aimlessly wandering around in the woods?" The inspector looked down at his feet and then at the crumpled car laying on its side. "Oh, dear God, no; don't let him be under the car."

At once he began barking out orders. "Joe, call the state prison and tell them to send their hounds down here, we may need them. You other men get over here; we're going to lay out a grid and do another search. If we don't find him this time, we will have to roll the car over. I hope it doesn't come to that; if he isn't dead already, rolling the car over could crush him." Even though his mind was on the rescue, the inspector had moments when his mind drifted back to his home and his little boy tucked in safe and sound in his little, blue room with his Pooh bear. "Come on guys, let's hustle; we've got to find that kid."

Chapter III

A t first James thought he was blind when he opened his eyes. Everything was so dark. Slowly, however, stars came into view and then trees. He thought he could smell the scent of pines, but for some reason he couldn't breathe well through his nose. Where was he, was he dreaming? If he were dreaming, it was the most real dream he had ever experienced. Why were his ears ringing? It was almost as if someone were ringing a bell inside his head. He lay still for a long time fearing to move about in this new world. Had he traveled like Alice through the looking glass? What could he be doing out in the woods and at night too? Slowly the ringing began to subside though never going completely away. He could hear another sound, one that he had heard before. He began to decipher the sound by sorting all the sounds that he had experienced through his thirteen years of life. "That's it," he thought, "my birthday party. But where is everyone else? There's that sound again but what is it? It's water; that's it, it's water, and boy would I like to have some right now!"

He tried to rub his eyes so that he could see better, but there was dirt and something else sticky all over his face. "Well," he thought, "at least there's water nearby so I can wash this off my face." Since he was lying face down, his first instinct was to push up with his hands and stand up, but he felt like something was pushing him down onto the ground. He strained to turn and see what was on him, but he couldn't see a thing. Then he tried to roll over; three times he tried but to no avail. Finally, by grabbing a pine sapling he tugged and pulled until he slowly rolled over.

After his tug of war with the pine sapling, James propped himself up on his elbows. Now that he was on his back, he had a better view of his legs. He was right; there was nothing laying on his legs, nothing at all. "Well, maybe my legs are broken," he said aloud. "But they don't hurt; maybe it's like when I cut my finger that time and had to have stitches. It didn't hurt then either, not for a little while, and then it was a killer. Well all this talk is getting me nowhere fast." The ringing in his head had almost gone away, but now his lip was beginning to sting. He reached up and touched his lip, and some of the grime came off on his fingers. Touching his lip caused it to hurt even more, and he jerked his hand away and winced with pain. He tried to see what was on his hand, but it was too dark to see very far in front of him. He decided it was time to try for that water.

He couldn't see the water, but he could hear it.

He tried his best to get to his feet, but his legs just would not cooperate. Then he decided to try and crawl but his legs wouldn't draw up into a crawling position. "These stupid legs," he thought, "I can't even crawl." He always had a fighting spirit, and he wasn't about to be whipped now. Putting two and two together, he worked out a system where he could pull himself by using his elbows and by pulling on saplings and rocks. Gradually he began to move; then with practice he began to pick up speed. Occasionally he paused to catch his breath and to get a new bearing on the stream. By the time he reached the stream he was exhausted and out of breath. He crawled right into the edge of the water and collapsed. Had the water not been ice cold he may have even drowned.

The stream was small, but it was wet and cold. It was also difficult to keep his hands from slipping on the smooth, round stones. Eventually he was able to prop on one elbow and cup water in his other hand. He splattered water on his face and in his eyes allowing it to drip off his chin and fall back into the stream. Had it been day-time, he would have seen the water changing into a bright rose color. He thought he had been hurting before, but he didn't know what hurting was until the cold water hit all the deep cuts on his face. It felt like there were a thousand needles sticking him in the face all at once. He winced and cried out with pain.

Eventually the worst pain subsided as he drank from the stream, but the pain was soon replaced by a terrible headache.

James lay down beside the little rambling stream and tried to sort out the situation. How was he going to get out of this? He thought back over the evening. He remembered traveling down the road and having the same old argument with Gin about those stupid seatbelts. "Maybe they weren't so stupid after all," James thought. He remembered a terrible crash followed by excruciating pain and then a feeling of being totally weightless. It kind of felt like the "free fall" at Six Flags. Then he remembered waking up on the ground.

How would he ever get out of this mess; he couldn't even walk with two broken legs? And where was everybody else? "Well," he said aloud," I can't walk, but I sure can talk. Help! Help! Help!" He yelled into the sea of blackness that surrounded him.

Inspector Johnson had sent his men back into the woods and had searched everywhere around the car and even in the trunk. For thirty yards they had crawled and looked under bushes, behind trees, everywhere they could think to look. They had dug around the edge of the car looking for clothing or a hand or anything that would indicate that the boy was under it. They had found nothing. "All right boys we're 'gonna' have to roll it!" yelled inspector Johnson.

They lined up on the hill behind the car and were about to push when Gabe yelled out, "Hold on there just a minute captain, listen!"

Gabe had spent many hours in the outdoors during his life. Instead of watching the American wilderness on television he had chosen rather to be a part of it. He learned that you can have an adventure just sitting outside at night listening to the night sounds while others fry their brains watching the "boob-tube" or "idiot box," as he preferred to call it.

While everyone else was scampering about going crazy, Gabe had been carefully looking around and listening to everything. Something had been troubling him about the whole scene, but he just couldn't put his finger on it. Gabe had a wisdom that is shared by few these days. He wasn't much for facts and figures, but he sure was good at putting two and two together. It was something about the car. He kept looking at it laying on its side, windows all broken out, glass all around the car - "That's it!" he mumbled. "Glass is all around the car except the back, and the back window is almost completely gone. But where is all the glass?" The glass had to come out some time before the car came to a stop, but after it left the road.

Quietly Gabe slipped back toward the highway

where the car had left the road. It wasn't that he wanted all the glory for finding the boy or that he didn't want any help. It was the simple fact that he didn't want all the "professionals" running around him destroying the trail. Now, Gabe was the hound that had just caught the scent.

In the chaos around the car one rookie cop saw Gabe walking off and reflected to another officer, "Look at that old country fool, out here where it ain't none of his business. Why don't the inspector just tell him to leave and get out of the way? He ain't done nothing since he's been here anyway."

Gabe began working his way back up the trail left by the car. Meticulously he worked his flashlight back and forth along the sides of the trail. Twice he thought he had found something, but both times the sightings turned out to be beer cans that had been discarded by a passing motorist. Then his eye caught the slightest twinkle off to the right. Slowly he raised his flashlight in the direction of the twinkle, and all at once the forest floor became a field of sparkling diamonds. There were twinkling shards of glass everywhere. Gabe looked at the sight and shook his head. "That boy must be dead to have broken that back window with force like that," he thought. However, after shining his light and not finding anyone or a body, he heard a noise.

It wasn't the noise that he heard, but the noise

that he didn't hear that bothered him. Every since he had arrived on the scene, the trickle of water could be heard in the background from the nearby stream. Now, however, the pattern in the streams melody had been altered. It was at this point that Gabe had hollered back for the others to be quiet and listen. Time and time again the orchestration of the stream was altered to play a new tune. Gabe walked slowly at first homing in on the sound. Faster now, almost at a trot so that by the time James hollered, "help," for the third time, Gabe was kneeling at his side.

James caught a flash of movement out of his left eye, and the next thing he knew he was looking into the face of his angel. From the reflection of the flashlight, James was able to see the silvery hair, the deep blue, kind eyes, and the tanned, furrowed skin of the old man, and James began to sob. He had forced himself to be brave until now; now James could let go, and he did.

Gabe had seen the tracks where James had dragged his legs on the way to the stream. He had also noticed his bleeding elbows and hands, which he had used to push and pull himself. Gabe would be the first one to tell you that he was not a doctor. Sometimes he was wrong, as he hoped he would be in this case. Before any X-rays or MRI'S were done, before the doctors told James' parents, "We've got a problem," Gabe knew what the end of this story would be. He had seen animals do the same thing but only seriously injured ones. Only one kind of injury caused an animal to drag itself this way.

Old Gabe knew the battle that lay ahead of James. As James sobbed, Gabe stroked the boy's matted hair, and with a tear glistening in the corner of his eye said, "It'll be all right son. Just you wait and see. It'll be all right. Over here boys," he yelled, "over here."

CHAPTER IV

At the hospital Gin was elated when she heard that her brother had been found. The nurses were keeping her informed as details came in. Her dad's condition was steadily improving, and he had stabilized. It was still touch-and-go with her mom. Her mom was still in surgery and was expected to be there at least two more hours. The doctors said that she came very close to death, but that every hour was a plus in her favor. They also said that if she made it through the night, she would probably live. Everyone had been so anxious with James missing that when word came that James had been found, all the nurses and staff on the floor cheered.

Within minutes though, the exaltation became despair, even worse than before. It was as though a black cloud had enveloped the entire floor of the hospital. Gin asked repeatedly, "Is James dead? Somebody tell me something, please!"

Everyone that Gin asked would say things like, "No darling, he's not dead; he'll be fine." But the expression on people's faces betrayed them.

Finally, the old matriarch of the hospital came

in and sat down on the edge of Gin's bed. She had a kind face that gave a motherly impression. In her white uniform with her silvery hair she looked like an angel who had just descended from heaven. She smiled warmly and her plump cheeks erased the thin wrinkles which had etched themselves into her face, "Gin, your mother is out of surgery. The doctor said that he would be in to see you in a few minutes. He knew you were anxious for some news. He said that your mother is stable and seems to be improving. He also said that barring any complications and if her condition continues to improve over the next twenty-four hours, she should have a one hundred percent recovery. In the meantime, she is in "guarded condition" and is being watched very carefully by our Intensive Care Nurses. They're the best in the business. I really believe that she will be fine. We just have to keep hoping and praying. Anyway, your dad is doing great. You two will probably be able to go home in a couple of days."

"Well, what about James? Is he alive? No one will tell me anything!"

"Yes, Gin, he is very much alive."

"You're not telling me everything though, I can tell."

"Well, Gin," she paused, "there have been some complications."

"What do you mean by complications?"

"Well, Gin, I'm not a doctor, and I don't know all there is to know about injuries and things like that. The doctors won't let us discuss patients' conditions until all the test are run and a complete diagnosis is made. Sometimes I really wish that I could tell patients what I think, but sometimes I am wrong, and things aren't what they appear to be."

"But you can talk to me about James, I won't tell anyone, I promise."

"James is on his way here, and you should be able to talk to him tomorrow."

"But I have to know—"

"Now dear," the nurse cut her off, "let's just get some rest and wait and see what the doctors say. As soon as I can find out something more definite, I'll try to get word to you. You need some rest now. I'm going to give you something to help you sleep. Now, you just turn your pretty head over and get some sleep."

"Yes mam," Gin said, looking more worried than ever.

By the time James arrived at the hospital, he was already hooked up to all kinds of IV'S and monitors. He was strapped down so tightly to the backboard that he couldn't move any part of his body.

When the ambulance pulled up at the emergency room, doctors and nurses swarmed all around him. They had been advised of the seriousness of his condition and were prepared to do battle in order to save his life. After determining that his vital signs were satisfactory, the medical staff sent James upstairs for X-rays and an MRI. Before any treatment could be continued, the doctors had to know the full extent of his injuries.

Gin caught a glimpse of him as he passed her door, but she didn't recognize him with all the straps and braces. However, she did notice the orderly pushing the gurney. As the orderly passed a nurse in the hallway, she looked questioningly at him. They never spoke a word but his eyes told the story as they passed. Slowly he shook his head from side to side. The orderly's gaze lasted only an instant, but the message was clearly received. Within minutes the party line had spread the news throughout the hospital.

In less than an hour, James found himself whisked away again, this time in a helicopter. He was kept fairly sedated and only awoke occasionally. About sixty-five minutes later, he landed two hundred miles away at the regional trauma center.

As he was rushed through the doors, he happened to overhear one of the doctors tell another,

"I talked to him before they left and told him that he may as well keep him there. But I'll do what I can."

When James finally awoke two days later, he still felt groggy. His nose itched like mad, but no matter how hard he tried, he couldn't raise his arm to scratch it. He tried to turn his head, but he couldn't turn it either. He tried to call out, but the words wouldn't come, and his eyes began to fill with tears. From somewhere behind him he heard a movement. As the nurse came into view, he found out that he had not only lost his patience, but now he had also lost his heart.

Just the sight of the nurse made James forget about the hospital, forget about his pain, forget everything. She was a goddess in white. Surely, he had died and gone to heaven. Now, James was a thirteen-year-old boy again. His heart raced in his chest; his breathing became shallow, and all his emotions were registered by the monitoring equipment which guarded the head of his bed.

Nurse Rachael, fairly new on staff, had transferred to the trauma center only a month ago after spending two years of training and duty in a local emergency room. As she floated around the end of the bed, James couldn't help but notice her beautiful, green eyes and her long, silky brown hair. Although she was at least ten years older than James, trying to convince a thirteen-year-old that he is too young for love is like telling birds not to fly.

"Welcome back," said Rachael.

To James, it was more like she sang the words as they echoed through the drab room. James savored and hung onto every syllable. Her words sounded just like he thought they would, like they would coming from someone as beautiful as she was.

Sadly, the deathly silence that ensued after the last syllable brought James back to the reality of his situation. Slowly the upturned curve on his face began to droop. He felt more like a machine than a boy. There were tubes in his arms, wires on his chest, and even tubes in his nose.

He wondered whether there were also tubes and wires on his legs. He was still lying flat with his head strapped down. He tried to lift his legs to see if they had wires and tubes too. But he couldn't move them. "Well," James thought, "I must be strapped down all over."

James only stared at and followed her with his eyes as she moved around the room.

"Oh, I'm so sorry. I haven't introduced myself." "I'm Nurse Rachael."

James continued to lay motionless and did not even acknowledge that she was talking to him.

"Hey, I'm talking to you! Anybody in there? Earth to James, come in. Are you there? Do you copy? Oh, my goodness, don't tell me I have the wrong room!"

Rachael checked the name tag on the door. "No, this is the right room, room 180."

"Oh, no! I just had a terrible thought; what if they sent me the wrong patient! Come on, James, I know you can talk. You were talking in your sleep. You are James, aren't you?"

Slowly James opened his mouth, "Yes it's me," he said.

"Well, it's about time you woke up. You've been asleep for almost thirty hours. Do you know how bored I get with no one to talk to?"

Before James could answer, the door flew open, and in strutted Dr. Fredericks.

"Good morning," the doctor said.

"Good morning Doc.," answered Rachael.

"How's our Prince Charming doing this morning?"

James blushed when he realized the doctor was referring to him in front of such a pretty girl.

"Well, at least he's awake. I was about to start calling him Sleeping Beauty."

Rachael responded, "His vitals are good, and if we can get him to eat something, maybe he'll start talking a little."

There was a knock at the door, but James could not turn his head to see who it was. He heard a sort of shuffling noise as someone hobbled over to his bed. Finally, he was able to see someone that resembled his dad. The person had several bandages on, and he was pretty scratched up and bruised. Gin was supporting one of his arms, and he had a cane in his other hand.

"Oh, son," his dad said as tears flooded his eyes. "I was so worried about you. You slept so long. The doctor said you'd be ok, that you just need time to rest, time to heal. You just wait and see; you'll be as good as ---"

James's dad's words trailed off as he coughed to try to cover up his mistake.

"Uh, Mr. Whitman, we have more tests that we can schedule now that James is awake. Then we can find out what we need to do to help him."

Gin stepped up, "James, I just don't know what I would do without a little brother to pick on; you just get tough and start fighting."

Gin bent over and kissed him on the forehead.

"Yuck," thought James.

"We'll go ahead and start those tests if it's ok with you, Mr. Whitman."

"Just the test we have already talked about, right Doc?"

"Yes, that's right."

"Why do I have to have any test?" mumbled James.

"Well, we just want to do everything we can to help you heal faster," said Dr. Fredericks.

"Well, I guess we had better get going," said his dad. "They told us we could only stay for a few minutes. Be a good boy and do all you can to help them. We'll see you later after your tests."

"Ok," said James.

"Bye," said Gin. "I'll see you later."

"Oh Gin, I need you to bring me something back," said James groggily.

"Sure, what do you need?"

"Some antiseptic for my forehead. This is totally gross. I can feel the germs growing from contact with sister lips."

Gin opened her mouth as if to say something mean but instead just said, "Yeah, ok."

James couldn't believe his ears; she didn't have a come-back.

"Something is definitely wrong. It's Mom," thought James.

"Where's mom?" yelled James. "She's dead, isn't she? And don't lie to me! I know she's dead. You are all acting strange, even Gin." His eyes were rapidly filling with tears.

"No, no, James she's not dead. Just settle down a little bit and let me talk to you," said Dr. Fredericks. "For a while we did think that we might lose her. Now she is doing great. She should be able to go home by next week."

"Dad," James paused, "I want to know the truth! I've got to know."

"James, you know I've never lied to you. You and me both shoot straight from the hip, don't we? We always have, and we always will. Mom's ok, I promise."

Doctor Fredericks followed them out the door and called Jim down the hall and into an empty room.

"Gin, we'll be out in a minute. Here's some change. How about getting us a Coke."

"Sure, Dad," said Gin. Now she was playing the little, obedient daughter role again.

"When will he let me grow up?" she thought. "Here I am, sixteen-years-old and I still can't listen to an adult conversation."

"Mr. Whitman, you are a very fortunate man," the doctor began. "You were in a terrible accident which should have killed your entire family. Well, maybe not Gin. You know she was the only one wearing a seatbelt. Your entire family must really have a guardian angel. With some time for healing and therapy—"

"Therapy for what; what are you getting at? Doc, you've been beating around the bush. What is it that you're not telling me? Is it James?"

"I'm," he paused, "I'm afraid it is. I put this off as long as possible. Probably longer than I should have, hoping that," another pause, "hoping for anything, any kind of good sign."

"James is paralyzed, isn't he?"

The doctor paused and took a deep breath.

"Yes, Jim, he is. I'm so sorry. I should have told you earlier. I was hoping the test were wrong or maybe I was wrong. I guess I was hoping for a miracle."

"But miracles like that just don't happen often, do they Doc? How bad is it?"

"We still have to determine that. There are a few more test to run."

Jim leaned back against the wall shaking his head in disbelief.

"Well, when should we tell James about this?"

"He'll figure it out pretty soon on his own," said the doctor.

The doctor scratched his balding head and then pulled on his beard as he contemplated the decision.

"I would say as soon as you feel the time is right. It will be soon. You will know when. When the time comes, I know some excellent therapy centers where you can take him."

"Doc, you've got to give me more to go on. Tell me, how bad do you think it is?"

"As I said earlier, the test we've done so far are inconclusive. However, I can tell you this for sure; James will never walk again."

Dr. Fredericks had a great deal more to say about therapy, braces, wheelchairs and other sanitary stuff that goes along with a hospital. But Jim didn't hear a word that the doctor had to say after saying that James would never walk again. In his mind, Jim was watching James as a toddler awkwardly taking his first steps. Then kicking a soccer ball down the field and finally rounding third base and sliding into home. It was as if Jim was lost in a dream. All he heard was the echoing in his head, "He'll never walk again, ---"

When he stepped into the hallway, Gin was standing there with two cokes in her hand. She stuck a Coke out to him and almost dropped it when her dad didn't reach for it.

"Dad, are you ok?" she asked.

"Yeah, uh, yes, I'm fine. Let's go home."

"Aren't we going to go back to say goodbye to James first?"

"No!" was all he abruptly replied.

They walked silently away, not speaking, not looking to the left or to the right. Two people, one confused and uncertain. The other, an empty hull, searching, looking for some sanity in this new, insane world.

CHAPTER V

They rode without talking for almost an hour. For what seemed like an eternity, Gin looked at the unopened Coke beside her dad. It just sat in the little, blue, plastic drink holder hanging from the door. It seemed they had had those old blue holders forever. She sat and daydreamed about the big argument which had resulted in buying the can holders.

James was only five when they bought the new car. For some unknown reason, buying a new car always propelled dads into making trips. Their trip, only a week after purchasing the new car, was to the beach. From the moment they departed, they were having a fantastic time. They sang songs, played games, and their mom told her famous adventure stories. Everything was going great until her mom opened the snacks and the cooler.

"Uh oh," said Dad. "Hold on there a minute, little lady, while we circle the wagons."

Everyone laughed because her dad did such a poor impression of John Wayne, but he of course thought he was great.

"No, don't pull over; we don't have time," said

Fran.

"Now Fran, we just got this car, and we'll be years paying for it."

"We'll be careful, and I'll help the kids. I tell you what, you watch the road, and I'll watch the kids, deal?"

Jim finally noticed that his left front tire had crossed over the centerline on the highway. Not wanting to admit that he had made a mistake, Jim conceded by saying, "All right, but be careful."

James, being a normal five-year old, was so excited about the trip that when Fran tried to hand him a Coke, he grabbed the cup too fast, and out the Coke flew in one great torrent covering himself and cascading down into the smallest crevices of the seat. Gin remembered he mother's screaming and her dad swerving all over the road and finally pulling off on the shoulder of the road.

What happened then made a violent, erupting volcano look like a fourth of July celebration. Her dad was yelling and screaming as he frantically tore through her mom's thoroughly organized and arranged picnic in the trunk. Finally, not finding any paper towels, he grabbed the red checked table cloth from the trunk and began soaking up the Coke.

"Well, this seat's ruined!" yelled Dad.

Mom had forgotten all about the Coke on the seat, she was staring at the interior of the demolished trunk. There were boxes and bags turned upside down, sideways, and every way but the right way. She had been so careful to pack everything so neatly. Not only were the picnic supplies stacked neatly, but also packed in the order they were to be used. She had put the picnic basket, which was also packed in the proper order, on bottom. The red checked table cloth was on top so that it could be taken out first and spread out in preparation for the food.

Mom got back into the car and sat motionless and noiseless. Inside, she was a raging inferno waiting to spread pain and destruction.

When Jim finished drying the stained seat, he hurled the tablecloth back into the trunk and then slammed the lid crushing several bags of chips in the process. He also slammed the car door as a repeat performance in case anyone missed the first episode. It seemed an eternity before anyone spoke. Jim just sat there breathing hard and Fran just sat and stared straight ahead.

James happened to be the victim who spoke first and ignited the fuse by asking, "Where's my drink?"

For a split-second Jim's and Fran's eyes met as they turned toward James and a violent confrontation ensued. First, their anger was directed at

James and then at each other. The argument went on and on and was about to crescendo when James burst into tears. Somehow, he knew he was responsible for all of this, and he didn't know how to stop or to fix it.

Gradually Jim and Fran calmed down, more concerned about James than the car seat. They debated about returning home, but self-guilt drove them onward toward the beach.

They stopped at a convenience store just outside the next town so that Jim could get something to clean the seat with. Fran was looking for paper towels, which she had forgotten to pack. Gin, in the meantime, tried to read all the funny keychains hanging on the display by the counter. Some were funny, but some didn't make any sense at all.

James just kind of ambled around the store picking up this and that and constantly being warned by his mother to put it back. Suddenly he squealed so loudly that even the store manager came running from around the counter to see what had happened.

In each hand James had one of the blue drink holders. "Look Mama! Look Mama! I'll never spill my drink again."

By this time the whole family had come running thinking that James was hurt. Of course, when they checked out at the register, Jim had to pay for four blue drink holders.

Gin was still looking at the blue drink holder on the door and thinking how long ago the incident had all happened. She turned to look at the seat, and surely enough she thought she could still see a faint sign of a stain. It didn't really matter though; that was eight years ago, and the seats had long ago been given up for loss. It was funny, she thought, how after two or three years they could eat or drink anything they wanted to in the car.

She was so deep in thought that she didn't realize that the car had stopped and that they were sitting in their driveway at home.

"Gin," Dad said, his chin was quivering. With all the strength he could muster, he said, "Gin, I've got to tell you something."

"What is it, Dad?"

Jim swallowed hard and looked straight at her. "It's James," he said. "James will never be able to walk again."

"Oh, that can't be true. He may have to stay in the hospital longer, or maybe he'll have to have therapy, but he will walk again. I just know he will. You wait and see."

"Gin, I talked to the doctor. He said that James' spinal cord was completely severed. There is no chance short of a miracle."

"But Dad, maybe another doctor or another hospital?"

"We just can't undo what has been done Gin."

"But Dad," Gin called through her tears.

An emotional flood of feelings enslaved them that afternoon. There was gratitude that James was still alive, the hate of what the accident had done to him, and the fear of the unknown future.

Gin walked slowly up the brick steps on the slope leading to the front door. "James can't do it" she said.

"What did you say?" responded her Dad.

"James can't do it."

"Can't do what?"

"Can't climb steps," said Gin.

"Hum, that will be a problem," said her Dad. "We'll have to come up with some kind of a solution. But I can't think about that right now."

By this time Gin had made it to the front door and was taking out the hidden key that they kept behind the mailbox.

"He can't do this either," said Gin.

"You mean reach the key," said her Dad.

"No, he will have to have a wheelchair."

"Gin, I realize that."

"But Dad, don't you see? He won't be able to get through the door."

"Oh, you're right. It's too narrow," he said scratching his neck nervously.

All afternoon Gin seemed to be preoccupied with finding different things that James would not be able to do. His wheelchair would not be able to go through any of the doors, especially the bathroom doors. He could not run, which meant forgetting baseball, football, basically everything.

Every time Gin thought of something new she shouted it to Jim who was trying to catch up on all of his work.

Jim thought to himself, "I really do not need this right now. I've got to get my mind off the accident for a while. Not off the accident," he thought, "off of him." But he thought, "As long as she is talking about it, then the conversation is probably good for her."

The clock struck two o'clock a.m. Gin lay in the dark staring at the ceiling. "He'll never date, get married, go to the prom, play badminton, ping pong,---"

CHAPTER VI

The early morning sun woke Fran as she fought to catch forty more winks. She had been restless all night. It was more than pain from the surgery and more than the nurses waking her to check her pulse and temperature. They even woke her one time because earlier she had requested something to make her sleep. She couldn't believe that they woke her up to give her a sleeping pill. Now, something else was beginning to bother her.

She knew that Jim and Gin were at home and that James was on the next floor. She had also requested many times that they put her in a wheelchair and take her to him. If they couldn't do that, then she asked that they bring him to her. She had made up her mind that this would be the day that she would see her son! And may God help anyone who stood in her way!

She heard a noise. There were footsteps and talking in the hallway growing louder with each step. She rolled over and pretended to be sleeping.

A nurse came in with a cafeteria worker who was carrying Fran's breakfast tray. They were whispering to one another, but it was hard to understand what they were saying. Fran caught only bits and pieces.

"Let her sleep," said the nurse. "She was awake most of the night, and she will need the rest."

"What about her son?" whispered the cafeteria worker. "He doesn't eat hardly any of his food."

"Well, you've got to understand the complications that resulted from his accident. He has to be hand fed; he can't get up and go to the restroom. Why, he can't even scratch his nose they have him so strapped down."

"That's it," Fran shouted! I've had it!"

Both of the ladies jumped as if someone had fired a gun.

"Fran looked the nurse square in the eyes and said, "I want a wheel chair. I want it beside my bed, and I want it right now!"

"Now, Mrs. Whitman, we must settle down."

"Settle down my foot! I'm going to see my son. You get me a wheel chair, or I'll go myself, even if I have to crawl."

The nurse turned to the cafeteria worker for assistance, but by this time the worker had deposited her tray and was halfway down the hall, headed briskly back to where she belonged.

"I'll tell you what, we'll make a deal," said the nurse. "You ask any questions that you have first. Then we'll ask James' doctor to come by and see you in the morning. If he says it's ok, I'll take you up to see James myself. Is that a deal?"

Fran thought for a second and figured it was a deal that she could live with.

"Ok," she said, "so far no one has told me anything. Let's see how you can do. Here's my first question: You said James is upstairs; where is he, what unit?"

"He is in the Neuro/Intensive Care Unit."

"Ok, now we are getting somewhere. And why is he there?"

"Well, you see, after the accident he was transferred here by helicopter, and you were transferred here after you stabilized from your surgery. You both had very serious injuries. As a matter of fact, you wouldn't have made it had you not had surgery immediately. This is not just a hospital; it's a regional trauma center. Because of your injuries, you have been kept pretty sedated for the last four days. Your husband and daughter have been here every day, but you slept most of the time."

Fran remembered Jim's being there, but he wouldn't tell her anything that she wanted to know, or was it all just a dream?

"Now is about the time that they usually come so they should be here any minute. Why don't you have some breakfast and----"

Fran interrupted, "You still have not answered my question. What is wrong with James?"

"Well, it would be better if his doctor talked to you." Spinning on her heels, Nurse Jenkins, taking advantage of the situation, almost ran for the door. "Let me see if I can catch him before he leaves the hospital."

Fran raised her hand to stop the nurse, but it was too late; she was gone. Alone in the room, Fran began to pick at something on her plate. It tasted like yellow rubber without salt. She assumed that it was supposed to be eggs. Her stomach told her that she was not up to eating and she pushed the food aside. No wonder the food service worker said that James wouldn't eat.

More footsteps were coming down the hall, and her door slowly began to open. In walked a funny little man with a balding head and a little goatee that sufficed for a beard. Instead of Ivan the terrible, he looked more like Ivan the elf.

"That's it," thought Fran. "He looks like one of Santa's little helpers." By the time he left, she no longer thought of him as Santa's little elf; elves usually bring joy.

"Good morning, Mrs. Whitman," said Dr. Fredericks with a thick accent.

Fran returned the greeting and nodded.

"I understand that you have some questions for me."

"Tell me about James."

"Exactly what is it that you want to know? I just left him. He seems to be doing fine."

"No, no, he's not fine!"

"Well his vital signs are good," said the doctor as his voice trailed off. "However, I do not believe it is his vital signs that you are referring to, is it Mrs. Whitman?"

Fran just kept staring and shaking her head, "No," as her eyes began to water.

The fatherly doctor walked over to her bed, sat down, and took her hand.

"Mrs. Whitman, we have many things to discuss about James, but I would rather wait until your husband were---"

As if given a cue, the hospital room door slowly opened as Jim hobbled into the room followed by Gin.

"Good morning, Jim and Gin, how are you this morning?"

"Fine, doctor, and you?"

"Fine, thank you."

The doctor tried to smile even though his excuse for not talking to Fran Whitman had just hobbled through the door.

"Fran and I were just talking about James. I'm glad you are here. If I could trouble you to step outside for a min---"

"Jim doesn't need to step outside, Doctor. Anything that you need to discuss with Jim can be discussed in front of me."

"Well, Fran, it's just that you have suffered so much already from the accident and then the surgery. I was just hoping to delay this until you were a little stronger. However, you seem to be stronger than I first estimated."

Gin was just proud that she was not asked to leave the room. Did they consider her an adult now? It really didn't matter. At least it was a step in the right direction.

The doctor reached over and took Fran's hand again.

"Fran, the only way I know to do this is to give you the worst and get it over with. James' life has been saved, and he will be able to leave the hospital one day, but he will not walk out. He will be in a wheelchair, and he will have to stay in that wheelchair for the rest of his life. There's no surgery, no therapy, nothing that will ever allow him to walk again."

Fran appeared stunned. "How can this be?" she thought. "Not James. He runs so fast. He likes basketball and football and soccer and ----. He can't live like this, he won't live like this." "I know," said Fran. "We'll take him to a specialist, or-or we'll take him to a faith healer. I saw one the other day on television."

"Fran, Fran," Jim said snapping her out of her trance. "Not accepting the truth won't do any good. It won't help James or us. We have to accept the fact, he'll never walk again."

In the back of his mind though, Jim still left a little room for hope.

"Jim, Fran, I wish I could have given you better news. In a minute I'll try to give you some further information about his treatment. Before I do, though, do you have any other questions?"

"No," said Fran. "Thank you for telling us the truth, but you know that you're wrong, don't you?"

The doctor didn't say a word nor did his expression change; he just waited and listened. So many times, over the years he had watched patients and family members in denial.

"James will walk again. I just know that he will," said Fran.

"Mrs. Whitman, I do indeed hope that you are right and I am wrong. But for now, we have to take it one day at a time. Let me see if I can outline the rest of James' treatment for you. James will be in the hospital for at least three or four more months. We'll give him about two weeks for his other injuries to heal. After two weeks, he will need to have more surgery."

"More surgery, what kind of surgery are you talking about?"

"Well, we will have to do back surgery to fuse his spine where it was broken."

"And that won't help him walk?"

"No, it won't. You see Fran, the spinal cord runs down the backbone. It acts like a powerline. It carries messages from the brain to the rest of the body and from the rest of the body back to the brain telling it what to do. James' spinal cord has been totally severed. It's like cutting a power line and having all the machines shut down. James is fortunate though. He will be a paraplegic and not a quadriplegic."

"What's that?" asked Gin.

"Well, a paraplegic just can't walk. However, he can still have use of his upper body and his arms. A quadriplegic, on the other hand, usually can't move anything except his or her head. James is very fortunate in this regard."

"Does James know yet?"

"No, Fran, he doesn't," said Jim.

"Well, when should we tell him?"

"The doctor says that we will know when the time is right."

"I understand that you want to go and see him, is that correct?" said the doctor as he gave a questioning look and shrugged his shoulders.

"You mean right now?" asked Fran nervously.

"Yes, right now."

"Well, now under the circumstances, I don't know. I don't know if I can face him in that kind of condition. What if he asks, you know, about walking?"

"Then, we'll tell him. If he asks, that means that he wants to know. We want him to trust us. We don't want to begin his treatment with a lie," said the doctor. "Then he would never trust us again."

"By the way, if you would like a second opinion, I'll be glad to recommend someone."

"Thanks doctor," said Jim.

"Later on, he will have to have one, last surgery to remove some of the sharp curves on his hip bones and maybe on his spine," said the doctor.

"Why would he need that done?" asked Gin rather boldly.

"It will make him more comfortable in a wheel chair and will lessen his chance of having bed sores."

Gin looked inquiringly back at the Doctor, "What are bed sores?"

"Well, Gin, they can be nasty, little irritations on the skin caused by lying down or sitting too much."

"Well, James doesn't really have much of a choice, does he?"

"No, Gin, he doesn't. But we have to do everything possible to help him. I know this is difficult for you. And this is not even the hard part. That will come after you go home from the hospital. There are most certainly physical scars. All of you will be deeply affected by this. But there will also be emotional scars to deal with as well. Some of those scars will not surface for months or maybe even years."

"I believe it would be a good idea to have one of our hospital counselors visit with you. You think about it and let me know. I'll be happy to make all the arrangements."

"Thank you for your concern Doc, but we won't be needing a counselor," said Jim.

"Just the same, the offer still stands if you ever

change your mind. I still need to finish with my rounds, why don't we all go up and check on James? Do you think you're up to it, Fran?"

"I really don't know, Doctor Fredericks. I really do want to see him. I just don't know how I'm going to deal with it. I don't want to upset him."

"Well, in a way he already is upset. He's been asking for you since he awoke from surgery. We have had a most difficult time convincing him that you are not dead."

"James can be stubborn. How did you ever convince him?"

"I hope you don't mind but James was so insistent and upset that we had to slip in the other day while you were asleep and take a picture to show him. You're right. He is a very stubborn young man. Let's just hope that he stays like that, and we can use that stubbornness to help him."

It was true that he had not finished his rounds. But the wise old doctor had an ulterior motive for having the Whitmans finish his rounds with him.

A wheel chair was requested, and they gently helped Fran into it. As they went through the door, Jim heard Fran mumble, "Dear God, you can't just leave him in a chair like this."

"I have a couple more patients to look in on the way to James' room," said the doctor. "They are just down the hall and won't take very long. If you're ready, let's go. Let's see. Jim, you and Gin have seen James three or four times, but you haven't seen him this morning, right?"

"That's right," said Jim.

"So, you haven't seen his new bed then?"

"New bed? I haven't heard anything about a new bed."

"Yes, it's a special bed for patients with spinal injuries. Patients with spinal injuries cannot be moved easily without causing more damage to the spine."

As they talked and walked and in Fran's case, rolled down the hallway, Fran was able to see into many of the rooms. Many of the patients were old and feeble, but some were very young. Many looked very sick and looked like they may never leave the hospital. All along the hallway you could hear the steady beep, beep, beep of heart monitors. The monitors stood firm at the head of each bed like a sentinel watching over its master.

They made a left turn and had to stop at two, large wooden doors. Above the doors written in large bold letters was "ONCOLOGY DEPARTMENT."

Gin whispered to her Dad, "What's oncology mean?"

"It means these are all patients with cancer."

After walking through the doors, they walked about fifty feet down the lustrous, tiled hallway and then took a right through two more wooden doors. Beside the doors was written "CHILDREN'S WING."

When the doors opened, Gin felt like Dorothy opening the door to the land of Oz. Everything was brilliant. The bright colors leaped into your soul and became part of you. There were pictures of flowers and animals everywhere. One wall was covered with special artwork done by the children who were in the ward. There was a continuous line of handprint paintings and every kind of drawing and artistry imaginable. Some were done in crayon; some with watercolors, and some with charcoal. The most unusual one was done with ketchup and mustard.

As they walked down the hallway, they came to a blank space in the artwork.

"Ah, Billy must be working on something new," said Doc.

"Who's Billy?" asked Gin.

"Billy is ten-years-old and he has cancer of the bone. I have worked on his case for some time because the cancer is in his backbone. He has been in and out of the hospital many times in the past five years. He was diagnosed when he was about five.

His parents noticed he wasn't growing at a normal rate and brought him in. Since I am a neurologist and a spinal specialist, I was assigned to his case. It has certainly been a struggle working with him. Not because he is difficult or causes trouble. It's just that he is such a special kid. I've never met anyone that doesn't like him. Last week he had a chemo treatment that really did him badly, worse than any he's ever had. I was really worried about him, and I guess my concern showed. Billy looked up and smiled and said in a feeble voice,' What's wrong, Doc?' He was more concerned about me than he was about himself. That's just the kind of kid he is. I can't wait for you to meet him. I'll have to ask him about his new project."

"Are all the patients here boys?" asked Gin.

"No, Gin. Why do you ask?"

"Well, as we went by the rooms, I noticed all the boys have stocking caps on, and I have not seen any girls."

"Gin, many of the patients you have seen are girls. You see, the chemotherapy that the children take makes all their hair fall out."

"Oh, I'm so sorry," said Gin.

"Me too, Gin, but chemotherapy is something they have to go through if they want to get better. The treatment is usually pretty tough on them to start with but since none of the other children have any hair either, after a while they just accept baldness as the norm. They hardly ever mention being bald again unless they are making a joke about it. Most of the kids that have been here for a while actually make a game of being bald. You have to be kind of inside the group though, or they won't let you in on the game. Do you see that little boy at the end of the hall? He's another good kid. Maybe we can get him to play with us a little. Here he comes. Let's see what kind of mood he is in first."

The doctor stuck his hand out to the approaching youngster.

"Hey, Lukas my man, 'gimmie' some skin. What's 'happenin'?"

"Not much, Dr. Fred."

"It's Friday, you know. Where have you been so early this morning?"

"Now Doc, you know where I go every Friday. I have been to get a haircut."

"You have. Well, let me see."

Lukas snatched off his green stocking cap to reveal a perfectly slick head.

"Hum," said the doctor, "Looks pretty good, but it could use a little more off the ears, and he didn't get the part straight again."

"Should I go ask for my money back?"

"I would if I were you."

Gin and her parents were speechless, yet they tried to force a smile.

"I'll tell you what though. If he 'don't' tighten up, I am going to quit going to him altogether," said Lukas.

"Atta boy, Luke. You straighten him out. We'll check 'ya' later, ok? We 'gotta' run."

The group started easing on down the hall leaving the little boy all alone with his bright green cap and a much bigger smile.

Lukas shouted once more as they headed down the hall, "Well if you need any help in surgery or anything, you know where to reach me, don't you, Doc?"

"Sure thing, buddy. You'll be the first one I'll call. See 'ya'!"

They rounded a corner, and the little boy was gone.

"Are all the kids like that?" asked Gin.

"You mean hairless, I presume? Most of them are somewhere in the three L's."

"What's that?" asked Jim.

"Losing it, lost it, or looking for it to come back."

"No," said Gin, "I mean his attitude."

"No, they aren't but I wish they were. He does have a good sense of humor, doesn't he? Around here you have to learn to laugh because you already know how to cry. Having cancer is of course hard on the kids, but you would be surprised. The kids usually take it better than the adults."

As they approached the nurses' station, one of the nurses looked up, and simultaneously the rest of the nurses did as well.

One nurse leaned over to another nurse and said, "Go find Barbara and tell her that he's here."

The nurse scooted out of the station as if her heels were on fire and disappeared down the hall.

Barbara had drawn the short straw on this occasion. She was one of the senior nurses on staff and had walked this road many times before. It was not a job that she relished, but it was one that she did well.

An aging brunette with a touch of silver in her hair rounded the corner of the hallway.

"Good morning," she said and added a grandmotherly smile for seasoning. "How are you folks doing this morning?"

Everyone smiled back and spoke, not just because they were kind but because she was the kind of person who could draw a smile out of you even when you felt your well of smiles was empty.

"Doc, please come with me. We need to talk."

Raising a finger, she motioned the doctor to come.

The doctor just shrugged his shoulders, turned to the Whitmans and said, "I'm sorry, I know you're in a hurry. I'll try not to be more than a minute."

As she passed through the nurses' station, she bent over and retrieved a blue piece of construction paper from under the counter. Then they disappeared around the corner leaving the Whitman family to small talk with the other nurses.

They had been gone less than two minutes when the nurse returned and headed straight for a patient's room without saying a word. Finally, after waiting about five more minutes, Dr. Fredericks walked around the corner.

"This way please," was all he said as he headed down the hall.

Gin was the first to notice that something was wrong. It was as if the doctor had lost some of the pep in his step. Jim noticed, too, that the doctor's eyes looked a little red and puffy. Fran didn't notice anything. She just wanted to get to James.

Jim was the first to speak.

"Doctor, nothing has happened to James has there?"

"No, not at all. Why do you ask?"

"Well, you just seem upset."

The doctor paused and turned to face the Whitmans.

"I guess I do owe you an explanation. When I met with the nurse awhile ago, she told me that last night Billy's temperature suddenly went up."

The doctor paused and swallowed hard, gaining strength.

"He had fought so long, and his little body was so tired. His heartbeat became rapid but his blood pressure began to drop. His heart tried to pump the pressure back up, but his little heart just couldn't take it anymore. His heart rate finally became erratic and just stopped. It all happened so fast that there was little they could do."

The doctor, unable to continue speaking, handed Jim the folded piece of blue construction paper which he held in his hand. It was Billy's picture that had been missing from the wall. Jim turned the paper over, and on the front was painted a big white house with sea gulls flying all around it. Upon looking closer, he could see little rings over the birds' heads. Jim then realized that the rings were halos.

"Billy knew," said the doctor.

The bottom of the page read, "To my 'bestest' friend, Dr. Fred."

Also, on the bottom were a few moist, dark spots.

All Jim could say was, "We may need that counselor after all."

CHAPTER VII

They left the children's ward and soon found themselves at two more large, wooden doors. Over the door was a sign that said, "Neuro/Intensive Care-only two visitors per hour, no children under 12."

Gin thought, "Well now, I'm old enough, but now I'm the odd man out."

"Hold on right here for a second, I'll be right back," said the doctor.

In less than a minute, he was back and ready to proceed with the mission.

"You remember the bed that I told you about? Well, it's special because the entire bed rotates. Patients in James' condition must be turned every couple of hours in order to prevent bed sores from developing. Right now, James is turned facing down, and he is almost awake. I put a mirror on the floor so that you can see his face better. Unfortunately, he has been in kind of a foul mood because he wants to be unstrapped so that he can go home. Are we all ready to go in?"

"All of us?" asked Gin.

"Yes, we'll bend the rules a little this time."

As they were about to open the door, it suddenly opened by itself, and a nurse came rushing out. She jumped back suddenly, having almost run into the Whitmans.

"And a good morning to you, Sugar Baby," Doctor Fredericks startlingly chuckled.

"Now, don't embarrass me like that doctor."

"I'm sorry. I mean, nurse Rachael. Her friends call her Sugar Baby as a nickname because she was reprimanded once for slipping sugar-baby candy in to the kids. It doesn't hurt either that it is her favorite candy."

"What's so wrong with that? I mean that's not such a bad thing to do is it?" Fran Whitman asked.

"Well, all of a sudden the sugar levels on tests went sky high, but only in one wing of the hospital. It didn't take long to find the culprit. She quickly became the kids' favorite nurse. One day I heard her rattle as she walked by. I noticed her pockets bulging and embarrassingly she pulled five more bags from her pockets. So now she's Sugar Baby to most of us around here."

Dr. Fredericks realized that Mrs. Whitman was becoming rather antsy by the way she was wringing her hands.

"I've done it again, haven't I? I'm always running my mouth off. Let's go see your boy," said the doctor.

Nurse Rachel stepped aside as she pushed the door back open. Jim pushed Fran's wheelchair right up next to James' bed. James was very groggy from the medicine that he had been given.

"James, James," his mother whispered.

At first, she received no response. Then slowly, with Fran watching his image in the mirror, his eyelids began to flicker.

"James, it's mom. I love you. Now open your eyes; come on, you can do it."

Several times he opened and closed them only to be prodded by his mother to wake up.

"Mom, is that you?" James mumbled.

Slowly his eyes began to open wider and wider.

"Yes, son it's me."

"Mom, are you, all right? I thought you were dead."

"Yes, son, I'm fine. I've been so worried about you, though. I told them they would have to bring me up here or I would crawl up here myself."

James had the faintest hint of a smile because he knew when his mom meant business.

"Here," said nurse Rachael, "Let me show you how we roll him over. It's time anyway and then you can talk better."

The bed kind of hummed somewhere deep inside and slowly began to rotate. James moaned a little as his weight shifted.

"Mom, make them take these straps off of me. I want to go home! I can't even move my arms. Please make them let my arms loose."

Fran Whitman looked pitifully at the doctor.

"Sorry, can't do it, not yet. That's why nurse Rachael and the night nurse stay with him. There is always someone here to get him anything he needs."

"Well, when can you take them off?" Fran asked.

"It could be longer, but probably in about two weeks."

"Two weeks!" yelled James, now with his eyes wide open. "I can't stay this way two more weeks. I 'gotta' get out of here. I want to go home!"

"Well, James," broke in Dr. Fredericks, "that's what we want, too. But you don't want to go home in a bed like this. We have some more things we have to do before you can go home. I promise we'll do them just as fast as we can. But you can help us, deal?'

James thought for a moment and seeing he was in no position to argue he figured he may as well go along.

"Deal," said James.

"We'll start by moving you into a private room tomorrow with a television, ok?"

"All right!" shouted James.

Deciding to leave on a positive note, Dr. Fredericks said, "Well, that's enough excitement for one day. Fran, we have to get you back to your room."

"If we must," said Fran.

Slowly, due to her injuries, Fran reached up and kissed two fingers. Then gently she reached up and placed them on James' cheek.

"I love you, son, and I'll see you tomorrow."

"Sure mom."

As they backed out of the door, James said, "Mom, I love you, too."

Then as the door slowly closed behind them, Gin stuck her head back in and said, "See 'ya,' dog breath."

James just as quickly responded, "After while crocodile smile, with your crocodile teeth."

The door slowly closed, and James thought to himself, "I'm glad things are getting back to normal."

Just as Dr. Fredericks promised, James was moved into a private room the next day. Over the next seven days James became quite adept at Wheel of Fortune, Jeopardy, and best of all, Family Double Dare. The rest of the Whitman family were in and out daily during the wait for the next surgery.

Finally, the day for the surgery arrived. Jim, Fran, and Gin were in James' room waiting for the orderlies to come and take James to the operating room. James had been very quiet all morning, which was understandable due to his being nervous about the surgery.

"Mom, am I going to die?"

"James, what kind of a question is that? Of course, you're not going to die. Do you think Dad and I would let them operate on you if we thought that would happen? No way! The reason we are doing this is so you can get better."

Then when they least expected it, James dropped the bomb they had feared the most. The Whitmans had hidden newspapers about the accident, asked all the nurses not to discuss it, and limited visitors to family in order to protect James from the truth.

James stared intently into his mother's eyes.

"Mom?"

"Yes, James."

"Will this operation fix me so that I can walk?"

With eyes that screamed for help, Fran turned to Jim. The silence seemed to last for an eternity. Finally, James turned to his father.

"Straight from the hip, remember Dad."

"James," he began, "Many things happen that we can't understand or explain. We can ask why or what if I'd done this or that."

"But-----Dad," James interrupted. James already knew the answer now, but he wanted to hear it for himself. "You still have not answered my question."

A tear formed in the corner of Jim's eye to match the one that was slowly making its way down James' cheek.

"No, James, even with the surgery, you'll never walk again."

For a long time, everyone just sat quietly. The words Jim had just spoken were like a boat anchor striking the muddy bottom of the deepest ocean; the words sinking and being engulfed in its murkiness.

James had thought for some time that he may be paralyzed although he hadn't made his thoughts known to anyone else. Anytime he had been ill growing up he usually kept it to himself. Unless his mom or dad happened to notice that he was acting funny, was unusually quiet, or didn't eat right, no one would have ever known that he was sick. Sometimes no one knew until James' color was not good or until one of his parents noticed that his forehead was warm when they kissed him every morning to wake him up.

James had never let his suspicions be known, but when the nurses rotated his bed every two hours, he noticed that he could feel pressure on his chest and his arms. But try as he may, he never felt any pressure on his waist or legs. Also, when the nurses or doctors touched or did anything with his legs or lower body, James could never feel any sensation. He would hear a nurse mention moving his leg or taking a bandage off but he never felt their touch. It was as if his waist and legs were not even there. He was beginning to feel like half a boy.

Finally, Jim opened his mouth to speak, but as he did, there was a knock at the door. Two orderlies walked in with big smiles and a gurney. "Time for a little ride, my man."

"Not yet," Fran jumped in. "He can't go right now."

"Well, everybody's down stairs waiting except the doctor, and he'll be there any minute."

"Please," begged Fran, "just five more minutes."

"Oh, all right, but just five more, and that's it."

"Thanks," said Jim.

The orderlies left the gurney and eased back out the door.

Jim cleared his throat and took a deep breath. "James, you have something very precious. You have your life. We could all have been killed in that wreck. If I could trade places with you, I would do it in a heartbeat, but I can't. James, you can't give up. I know things look bad right now, but you can't just give up and quit on life."

If James could have turned his head and looked away, he would have. But his head was still strapped down, so he just closed his eyes.

Gin spoke up, "James, you 'gotta' be tough, like the coach says." Gin thought about what she said and wondered if she had said the wrong thing. She knew that mentioning the coach would remind James of baseball and that baseball would remind him of running. Then they would be right back to square one. She would have to be more careful with what she said in the future.

"James, I can't promise you what tomorrow will bring. But if you give up and die here like this, in this bed, then all your dreams and hopes and plans for the future will be gone."

"But don't you see Dad; they're already gone. I'll never play ball again. I'll never run in the park again. I'll be a weirdo, a clown, something that everybody will point at and stare, and laugh at." James cut his eyes away from his family and squinched his eyes shut, forcing the pools of water that had collected there to stream down his cheeks.

"Why God would let something like this happen I don't know," said Jim. "I can't understand it. All I know is there will be a tomorrow, and if you will let us, we'll face it with you. We'll help you, James. You'll see, something good will come of this, even though we can't see it now, I promise. But you have to be a fighter and not a quitter, right son?"

James relaxed his eyes, and the lines around them faded away. The muscles in his cheeks gradually reclaimed their normal position and slowly he opened his eyes.

"Right Dad," said James. Even though Jim wasn't convinced of James' sincerity, he took his thumb and wiped the tears from James' face.

"We'll be with you all the way son. You can do this."

James feigned a smile.

The door creaked once as it began to swing open into the room once again. One of the orderlies stuck his head into the room. "Last train pulls out in one minute." "All aboard," said the other orderly. " 'Gotta' go this time, my man."

Fran, Jim, and Gin all gave James a peck on the cheek. James let out a sorrowful moan as Gin approached. "Just remember, I'm already sick," said James.

The orderlies carefully released the cables that held James' bed in place. James preferred to call it the rack. He said it probably came out of an old castle dungeon somewhere. Carefully they placed James, along with part of the bed on the gurney and then headed for the door. The last orderly turned and said, "You can stay here or go to the waiting room beside the operating room downstairs."

"Thanks," said Jim.

As the orderlies headed out the door James mumbled something and they stopped to see what he had said.

"What was that my man?" said one orderly.

"Nothing, nothing really," said James.

"Well I know I heard you say something and something ain't nothing James," said the orderly in charge.

"What I said was, "Here goes nothing," said James.

"What's that supposed to mean?"

"Nothing, nothing really. It is just a saying, 'Here goes nothing'."

The other orderly shrugged his shoulders, "whatever," he said and headed down the hallway.

"Yep, that's right," thought James, "whatever." "Here goes nothing," again thought James. "Just a piece of meat on wheels, a nothing."

James could not even see where he was going, only the lights passing rhythmically one by one overhead. Faces, he saw faces as people passed by on their way somewhere. He saw faces with expressions of pity, faces of concern, and faces that said, "I'm glad that's not me." Then there were the smells; medical smells of alcohol and urine. Once he even smelled baked bread and fried chicken and he knew the cafeteria must be just down the hallway they had just passed. There were also bumps on the floor where the different sections of flooring met. Rhythmically and mathematically, each bump resounded. The orderlies maintained such a steady pace that he became quite adept at counting between the bumps; one, two, three, four "bump," one, two, three, four "bump," one, two, three-------. The only time the cadence changed was when they turned corners.

One of the orderlies touched a button on the wall after pausing their journey. A blast of cold air hit him and one orderly announced, "Here we are young man. We'll turn you over now to these other good folks who are going to take great care of you."

One of the nurses grabbed a chart off his bed, "You must be James she said." "We are going to take good care of you young man. First, we'll hook you up to some monitors and then we'll give you a nice warm blanket. I'll bet that will feel good." James thought, "sure, only from my waist up."

The next thing he knew another man with a mask on sat at his head and said, "James, I'm going to give you something to breathe and you may start to feel a little funny. Again, James thought, "you mean funnier than I do already."

"There you go," said the anesthesiologist. "Take some deep breaths."

James said, "I don't feel anything. I, I don't smell anything. I feel nothing. I am nothing."

CHAPTER VIII

The Whitmans decided they wanted to be as close to James as possible, so they went to the waiting room next to the operating room. When they entered the room, there was already an elderly man sitting back in the far corner of the waiting room. Gin thought he kind of looked like somebody's grandfather. Except for being a little heavy in the middle, the old man looked like he was in pretty good shape for a man of his age. He was well tanned from working out in the sun, and his tan made his white hair look almost silvery.

As they found a seat, they exchanged the usual pleasantries. Jim whispered to Fran, "He must have a wife in surgery."

After they had sat for twenty minutes and flipped through several well-used magazines, Jim happened to look up, and the old man's eyes met his. "Is your wife having surgery?" Jim asked.

The old man sort of smiled and said, "Nope. Just a friend," and that was the end of the conversation.

Seeing that the gentleman wasn't much of a talker, Jim just left him alone. "Either he doesn't have much of a personality or he really has something on his mind," thought Jim. "Anyway, he wasn't bothering anyone. Might as well just leave him to himself."

Most of the time the man just sat quietly with his forehead resting on his fist. Sometimes he would get so quiet they thought he may be asleep. Occasionally, though, he would mumble something or shift a little in his seat in order to keep the blood flowing.

For two hours the Whitmans sat watching TV and making small talk. Finally, after the third cup of stale coffee, Dr. Fredericks entered the room. Immediately the Whitmans were on their feet.

"Everything went fine and James was just taken up to recovery. I'm afraid my original prognosis was correct. His spinal cord was totally severed."

Gin had noticed that as the doctor entered the room, she saw the old man look up. He was looking at the doctor and for a second, she stared into the man's sky-blue eyes and saw only love and concern. By the look of his road-map face, he had been around for a long time. You could tell that he wasn't a newcomer to hard times. He was obviously a veteran of many tough battles. For a moment Gin thought, "I know this man. I know I've seen him somewhere before." Suddenly she realized that the doctor was still talking about James, and she redirected her attention to the present matter forgetting all about the old man.

After the doctor left, Gin once again turned toward the old man, but he was gone. She scanned the room, but he was nowhere to be found. Quickly she stepped into the hallway scanning both directions, but he had vanished. "I wonder who his friend was? Oh, well" thought Gin, shrugging her shoulders and sighing to herself. Slowly she turned and closed the door. She hoped that she and her parents could have a few moments without all the hospital sounds that she had grown so tired of hearing.

As the door's latch snapped securely into its housing, a thin wisp of silvery hair began to emerge from inside the door of the next darkened room. Seeing that the coast was clear, the old man took a few moments to raise his eyes upwards. Anyone passing by would have thought that he was just a looney old man. The old man didn't recite from a noted soliloquy, nor did he draw from some great oratory. He simply said as if talking to an old friend, "Thank you again, God. I can always depend on you." Then silently he slipped away into the next group of people that passed by, and for a time, into obscurity.

CHAPTER IX

The Whitmans all went back up to James' room to wait on him to return. Twenty minutes later, the phone rang, and it was one of the nurses in the recovery room. "I was just going to let you know that James is stable and doing fine. He will be down here for at least two more hours if you folks want to go and get a bite to eat. Just make sure and call back and give us a number where we can reach you if we need too."

Jim went ahead and left the number of a little sandwich shop just around the corner. He also left the nurse instructions that if there was any change in his condition, no matter how minor, they were to call them immediately.

James continued to improve, and after a week he was put into a regular bed without any straps. His attitude was improving some, and that made everyone happier. Fran had been released from the hospital about two days before James' surgery. All three family members took turns staying with James. Some relatives had come from out of town, but since they were so far from home, very few relatives were able to come. The pastor at the new church they attended had made the long trek several times to see and pray with them.

It seemed like an eternity since the accident. They had all decided that time passes more slowly in hospitals and that if time every does stand still, its inception will be with a hospital clock.

A physical therapist came by every day for about thirty minutes and had James do several upper body exercises. She also guided him and his family in doing several lower body exercises to keep his muscles in shape and to prevent any further deterioration.

The second surgery came and went with no major mishaps, and finally Dr. Fredericks walked in one day with the news they had been waiting for.

There was a light tapping on the door, and for the two-thousandth time an "elf like" little man slipped into the room. "James," he said, "I think I have some news that you have been waiting on for a while. Unless unforeseen complications arise, Thursday can be your day to celebrate by going home. How's that sound?" It was ironic that Thursday was exactly four months since the accident had happened.

While James was excited about going home, the news brought new fears and concerns that James had never considered before to the surface. What would his friends think of him? Would he have to go to school? How would he ever be able to go to the bathroom at school? How could he carry his lunch tray? How could he get on the bus?

"I don't want to go," James said to his mother that afternoon.

"What's that, son?"

"I said, I don't want to go. I don't want to leave the hospital."

"James, you have got to be kidding. You know that you don't want to stay here!"

Over the last two months James' world had been turned upside down completely. Now his new world was the hospital. Leaving the hospital would be akin to being born again or reborn into another world. He was scared. Here he had friends, people who would help him, people who cared about him, people who would not laugh at him or make fun of him. Here he was safe.

"James, we must go home. Your treatment here is finished. There's nothing more they can do for you. The counselor said that now you are the general and fighting this battle is up to you. Your Dad will be here to pick us up first thing Thursday morning.

"Whatever," James said. "For a general, I sure don't have much say-so in anything."

For a long time, he was very despondent. But for some reason, over and over in his head he kept hearing the same words, "It'll be all right, son. Just you wait and see. It'll be all right."

The Wednesday morning sun brought not only daylight but also more nervousness and irritability for James. He spent a very restless last night in his sanctuary. His father arrived very early the next morning as promised. Nurse Rachael, who had not been his nurse since he was transferred to a private room, came to his room for the special occasion. When she walked into the room, James' spirits automatically improved.

"Good morning, Sugar Baby," he said.

"And a good morning to you, too. Well, today is the day, the one we've been waiting for. Are you ready?"

James' spirits dropped a little when he realized that he might never see her again. But they say that paraplegics can learn to drive. "If they won't bring me, one day I'll be back on my own," he thought.

Two orderlies lifted him into a wheelchair, and the task of dealing with James once again passed to Nurse Rachael.

"Here we go. Don't look back. Always look forward," said the young nurse.

As they walked out the door and turned the corner, they found a fifty-foot line of nurses, doctors, orderlies, and even other patients on each side of the hall cheering for James. Some of the nurses and doctors even came in on their day off just for the big send-off. They had all followed the whole story from beginning to the end. As he made his way down the hall, they were all cheering and patting him on the back. Even though James had his bad moments, as was expected, he was quick-witted with a good sense of humor. It didn't take long for everyone to get to like and to love him. He used to accuse the orderlies of keeping the bed pans in the refrigerator. These same orderlies were at the end of the line standing at attention.

They looked like a little hospital army standing there in their green uniforms. All of them were lined up against the walls with their backs straight and their shoulders squared. James didn't know it, but they had one special treat still in store for him. Each orderly acted as if he were a member of a precision drill team. It was obvious that they had been practicing their drill. As Rachael and James approached the first orderly, the lead orderly yelled, "Attention," and each orderly shoved a bed pan high in the air forming an arch for them to pass under. James was beaming from ear to ear. Never had anyone in the history of the hospital had such a send-off.

As they passed under each pair of orderlies, the bed pans were simultaneously dumped over them releasing hundreds of pieces of confetti cut from old computer paper. As Rachael backed him into the elevator, all the entourage began to clap again, and James gave them a "thumbs up."

Rachael and James traveled down to the first floor and out the front door trailing and dropping confetti behind them. While it was a great day for James it was the worst day ever for the house-keeping department. The cleaning staff grumbled and complained all day because someone had scattered paper throughout the hospital.

Outside the front door, under the shaded canopy sat a long, sleek black limousine. A tall, slender, uniformed driver stood beside it. "Your car sir," he announced as he opened the rear door.

James' departure from the hospital that day was unusual to say the least. One aspect however was significantly different, most patients climb into a car and leave the wheelchair behind forever. In James' case, the chair was neatly folded and stored in the trunk of the limo. The chair was forever destined to be an extension and a part of James.

The two-hour drive was something James had not thought much about, but it was wonderful. It had been so long since he had seen clouds and grass and trees and cows and everything that passed through the panorama before him. He watched and soaked it all in, thinking how good it was just to be alive. He considered the money that his mom and dad had to spend on the limo, extra money that they didn't have to spend. But he knew they wanted his homecoming to be special, and the expense was just their way of showing their love. They loved him more than they did their money. He felt warm inside. Little did he know of the battles that lay ahead.

As they pulled into town, there were no bands playing or banners flying. After all, they had lived there only a few short months and very few people knew them. He did see a few heads turning, but he knew that their attention was just because of the limousine and not who was riding inside. "Probably someone important inside," James imagined they were thinking. "But, no, no one important is inside, it's just me," thought James.

As they neared the last turn before their street, James saw someone standing on the corner. He was an older man, but he didn't look like an old man. He was tall, and he had hair that looked like silver. As the limousine passed, James watched him carefully. The stranger followed the limo with his eyes all the way down the street until it turned into the driveway.

To James, he seemed almost like a vision. There was something familiar about him, though something from way back in the past. Had James seen him before or perhaps seen a picture of him somewhere? He kind of looked like that movie star Jimmy somebody, what was his name, "Jimmy Stewart, that's it," James thought! But it can't be him. He just looks like him.

The car came to a stop, and for the first time in months, since that dreadful night, James looked upon his home. He leaned forward and backward as much as his seat belt would allow but he could not see the man anymore. The street corner was empty now. James tried to hurry his dad to get him out of the car, but his words were lost in a sea of noise caused by an old pickup truck without a muffler which passed behind them. The truck was so loud James could make out just the last few words of his dad's sentence, " 'Oughta' lock up people like that. What did you say James?"

"Never mind, Dad, it was nothing," said James as he watched the old pickup turn the corner at the end of the street and disappear behind the trees.

CHAPTER X

"**I**t is good to be home," thought James. "No matter what shape you're in, home is always a special place." As soon as he looked around, he realized some big changes had been made. A large pine tree had been cut down, and in its place a long ramp had been built onto the front porch. "Yes," he thought, "everything is ready. Everything is neat and tidy and ready for the cripple." For the first time in weeks, a real feeling of despair began to cast a shadow over him.

His dad broke his chain of thought. "James, we'll have to carry you inside for now. We have done a lot of work around here, but we haven't had a chance to widen the front door yet. We'll take care of it now that we are home."

"Sure, that's fine," said James. "But if you don't feel like carrying me, you can just dump me out and I'll crawl in myself," said James curtly. Jim and Fran looked at each other wondering what they had done to bring this on, but elected not to say anything and to just let it pass.

Jim cradled James in his arms and gingerly carried him inside to the sofa. He laid him down carefully and propped him up with some pillows. Then Jim turned on the TV, handed James the remote, and left the room. "That's it," thought James, "put the invalid to bed and turn on the babysitter. Don't worry, he'll be fine. Let him watch TV and keep him out of the way."

But James wasn't just fine. Any other time in his life if someone had told him to sit down and watch TV, he would have thought he had died and gone to heaven. Before, it would have been, "clean up your room, pick up your toys, take out the trash, do this, do that."

"Maybe," thought James, "it would have been better if I had died." He had seen enough TV in the hospital to last him a lifetime. In his heart, he really knew that his mom and dad just wanted him to feel loved and cared for. Then why did he feel so angry and frustrated? He knew there was something missing in his life, but he didn't know what. There was this feeling of emptiness that he really couldn't explain. He felt like a hollow shell, useless. It was the same feeling we all have at some point in our lives, to know that we matter, that we make a difference and that the world is a better place because we are here. At the time, one of the things he was missing was the need to be needed. He needed to feel wanted, to know that he made a difference and that he was an important part of the family. The first few days at home really turned into a struggle. When Fran cooked James' favorite meals, he would not eat well. He would just sit and play with his food. Before the end of his meal he usually grew bored and assumed the role of chemist and started mixing the different foods together. When he first started James would cut his eyes around the room just to see who was watching and for their reaction. Gin usually reacted first with, "gross Mom, make him stop." Fran would usually just shush her and tell her to eat her dinner. Nothing was really said at first, but when James graduated to mixing mashed potatoes in his tea with an added touch of ketchup and mustard, he made everyone sick. When anyone said anything to correct him, he always shot back defensively with a smart remark. It got to the point where no one wanted to eat with him anymore. They would slip a quick bite here and there, and when supper time rolled around, no one was hungry.

After a time, playing with his food also became old to James and he graduated to "accidently" turning over his tea or spilling his soup. Sometimes when their backs were turned, his whole plate would go crashing to the floor. Of course, one or all of them would jump up and say, "I'll get it. It's ok James. Don't worry about it." Once, while Fran was cleaning up the floor, a whole coconut pie came crashing down on top of her head, upside down of course. If looks could have killed, there would have been a memorial service the following day. Reluctantly they carried him back to Doctor Fredericks fearing that maybe there was more nerve damage than originally diagnosed.

Doctor Fredericks ran more tests and after several days at the hospital, the original results were confirmed. Finally, the spilling and turning over stopped. Much to Jim and Fran's dismay, the situation dramatically worsened.

It was James who proved beyond a shadow of a doubt that he did not suffer any further nerve damage. He also did it without any additional hospital charges. Instead of spilling or turning over his food, James created his own game of, "Food fighting for individuals."

After a heated private discussion, Jim and Fran had decided to give James only plastic dinnerware. Their discussion was a result of James having missled one of his mom's favorite pieces of fine china into the sink. At one time it was a piece of fine china; now it was only broken dreams sealed in a zip-loc bag in the bottom of the china cabinet.

James adapted and became quite adept at hitting the sink with plastic plates and glasses. Eventually, James graduated to the status of "Throwing Champion of the World," as he called himself. He could make all five of his mom's copper gelatin moulds hanging on the wall ring like a bell at a county fair. When he finished his dinner, he would drain his glass in his plate and then take the ice cubes and "Ping," the bright, copper moulds. If he sat on the right side of the table, he could side arm them and make them fall off the wall and into the sink. Finally, Fran refused to give James ice in his drink. She decided it would be much safer just to chill his drink in the fridge ahead of time. The first night Fran did so, James became infuriated and demanded to have ice in his drink. He received a firm, "No," and for the first time in a long time he ate more normally. "So that's the way it's going to be," he thought! "It's me against them now."

Being the resourceful young man that he was, it didn't take long for James to find an answer to his dilemma. At lunch the next day before he touched any of his food, he immediately drained his glass. His mom said sweetly, "My, you must have been thirsty."

Without saying a word, he allowed a wicked smile to caress his lips then turned and hurled the Tupperware glass at the gelatin moulds. He scored a triple, knocking three of the five moulds crashing into the sink. James yelled, "And the crowd goes wild!" as he yelled and swung his arms frantically around in triumph. Then, glaring at his mom, he grabbed his plastic plate, still full of untouched food, and sent it sailing like a frisbee toward the other imagined, alien, copper people hovering on the wall next to the fridge. Food was ejected from the plate as it neared its alien target. Now instead of decorative gelatin moulds, spaghetti sauce adorned the wall where the copper, alien invaders had previously been resting. James held his spoon up to his mouth, "This is your captain speaking, the enemy has been destroyed." Once again, James slowly turned his attention to his mother as he stared into her eyes. "You may now return to your normal operating procedures."

James' behavior was anything but normal for Fran. She just couldn't take it anymore. She burst into tears and ran from the room. As she ran down the hall, she could hear James laughing wickedly back in the kitchen. "Yes, indeed," he shouted. "The enemy has been completely destroyed." The laughter was the kind of gut-wrenching evil laugh which brings about complete humility. Life had become unbearable, and for a moment Fran allowed herself to wonder what it would have been like if the results of the wreck had been different. Fran locked herself in her room searching for any form of peace, a peace that was far removed from her tortured mind.

When Jim walked through the front door, Fran almost tackled him. It was quite obvious that she was visibly shaken. Taking his first look around after walking in told him why. The house looked as if it had been used as a set for a horror picture. It appeared that some demonic force had been released in their home and had totally obliterated it. Every houseplant had been dumped and thrown across the floor. Magazines and cushions from the furniture were scattered all over. Lamp shades were crooked and bent, and the pictures on the walls had been rearranged and now hung diagonally. The outside of the house looked normal enough. It gave no indication of the fury of the storm that had raged within as Jim had parked and strode happily inside.

Gin wasn't anywhere to be seen. She had gotten to the point where she stayed over at friends' homes more than she stayed at home. Her friends hardly ever came over anymore. James would always humiliate them by saying things like, "Oh, you've come to see the cripple huh or how many blonds does it take to push a wheelchair? Three, one to guide and one to turn each wheel."

James' physical appearance had degenerated to match his attitude. Jim and Fran encouraged him to be independent and to take care of himself. He rarely bathed and even more seldomly brushed his teeth. Neither could he be accused of being caught with a comb in his hair. Finally, he stopped changing clothes and wore and slept in the same clothes for days. They could usually determine if James had recently been in a room by the repulsive odor that seemed to hover and linger long after he had left.

Jim and Fran didn't know what to do. They started taking James to a counselor on a regular basis, but little improvement could be seen. Jim had even thought about spanking James, but he just couldn't bring himself to do it. He felt like James had suffered enough, and he didn't want to add to his pain. They had taken other things from him like his Nintendo 64 and his TV. Although James had been home for less than five weeks, his counselor suggested that maybe it was time to try to get him back into school, part time anyway. Fran felt that perhaps it was the idea of going back to school that had triggered this latest episode of violent behavior.

Jim panned the room. "Look at this mess," he shouted. It literally did look like a tornado had hit it. "At least nothing was broken," he thought. Then his eyes saw a twinkle coming from under a plant. It was his baseball trophy. The one he had received when he had coached James' team. They had won first place in the S.E. district and placed second in the state. Now it lay in six separate pieces scattered about the floor. The staunch, little man on top had been snapped off from his platform. Then each limb and finally his head had been wrenched from his golden body.

"James!" Jim yelled. The house resounded the

call, but no answer returned. Gallantly he marched off in search of his prey. After scanning three rooms, he found James in his own room seated in his wheelchair. As he dashed around the corner of the doorway, Jim almost ran over James. Jim was so mad that he drew his right hand back over his left shoulder and started his downward swing to back-hand James across the face. Suddenly Jim's muscles wilted, and he unfurrowed his brow as his vision began to clear.

Sitting slouched down in his wheelchair, James clutched his teddy bear. It was the same one they had given him for Christmas when he was only one year old and the one that his daddy had given him each night when he tucked him in as a toddler. Time was frozen. Finally, wilting, with his head hanging low, Jim sulked from the room. Jim couldn't see the smirk that spread across James' face after he left. The master manipulator had won!

James tossed the useless bear into the corner. A major victory had been achieved, the enemy vanquished. Now he was fully in charge. He liked it!

CHAPTER XI

Jim might have missed the sadistic expression on James' face, but Gin didn't as she marched into his room. She had met her dad in the hallway. When she spoke to him, he just had a blank look on his face and mumbled something as they passed each other in the hallway. James hadn't noticed her footsteps because he thought they were his dad's as he was leaving. When Gin rounded the corner, James had an impish grin on his face from ear to ear.

"What did you do, you little jerk?" she yelled. "You're responsible for all this mess, and who do you think gets to clean it all up? Me! That's who! Who cleaned it up yesterday and the day before? Me, and I'm tired of it! Everybody else may feel sorry for you, but I don't. I don't care if you rot in that wheelchair!"

James had sat quietly up until this point and just stared at his enraged sister. Gin opened her mouth to say something else, but he cut her off. "And guess who's going to clean it up tomorrow and the day after that. You, that's who!" he sneered.

Before she realized what she was doing, Gin

drew back and slapped James across the face so hard that it could be heard at the other end of the house. Slowly, he turned his face back around to face her. She didn't know what to expect. Inside she was shaking; she didn't realize she was trembling on the outside as well. Her hand burned from the impact. As he turned his head, whelps could be seen starting to form in the shape of a hand and fingers, her fingers. How had she done it? Why did she let him make her lose her self-control?

"And I expect it to be kept clean and dusted," he added without even a blink. Gin raised her arms with clinched fist and began to shake violently. She was about to become airborne for the attack when her mother entered the room.

Fran walked quietly into the room, took Gin by the arm and quickly escorted her back through the door. As Fran closed the door, a surly voice called back, "Remember, clean and dusted, every day." The comment was accented with a vile laugh so wicked that it didn't even sound like her brother anymore. It sounded more like a fiend from a cheap horror movie.

As the door clicked shut, Fran motioned for Gin to follow her to her room. She told Gin to have a seat on the bed, and then Fran sat down next to her. Gin was still shaking and was still very visibly upset. Tears streamed down her face. With the back of her hand she smeared a mixture of tears and mascara across her cheeks. She appeared to have on war paint.

"Gin, I'm not asking you to agree with me, but I am asking you to try and understand. James is terribly frustrated right now. You have your whole life ahead of you; you can do practically anything you want to. James has just had about every door of any future slammed in his face. There are many things that he will never be able to do. Unlike yours, his future is very bleak."

"But it doesn't have to be mom. He's just giving up. He's quitting everything; he's quitting life, and you're letting him. He's not doing all those things because he can't help it. James is just being mean."

"Gin, don't say things like that."

"Well it's true, and you and dad are letting him get away with it. My friends won't come over anymore; the house is a wreck, and I hate what he's done to you and dad."

"What do you mean by that?" Fran asked defensively while leaning back away from Gin.

"Well, you and dad don't even talk anymore unless you're fighting. We never go anywhere or do anything. We've even stopped going to church. For once, I'd like to go to a restaurant or a movie like we used to as a family."

"Well Gin, you're just going to have to be more

understanding."

"Oh, I understand him all right. I understand him too well. He ought to be put in a home or someplace for people like him."

"Gin, you act like you hate him or something!"

"I do, I do hate him! I wish he was gone. I wish I was gone!" Gin leapt to her feet, ran out the door, and burst into tears. Fran yelled for her to come back, but it was too late. She heard the front door open, but she never heard it close. Fran knew that Gin was gone. She hoped that Jim was still in the house and had not retreated like their daughter.

Up until this point, she had only felt frustration and helplessness. Down the hall she heard James' door creak slowly open. In her mind she could picture his glaring eyes peering through the small gap formed by the open door. She wasn't just afraid anymore; she was terrified!

CHAPTER XII

Just as Fran had suspected, Gin had fled to her best friend's house down the street. They didn't hear anything for about two hours. Finally, the telephone rang; it was Gin. She called to say how sorry she was that she had yelled and lost her temper. Gin said that she needed some time to get away for a few days and asked whether it would be all right for her to stay at Susan's until Sunday. Fran discussed the situation with Susan's mother, and they decided that considering the circumstances it probably would be best.

Fran was still on the phone, and Jim had gone to the store when she was interrupted by a perfectly dreadful noise. "My goodness, what in the world was that?" asked Fran. "Let me go, Judy, and see what's happening. I just heard a terrible noise in the front yard. I'll call you later, ok?"

"That will be fine, but call me back if there's a problem."

"Sure, I'll talk to you later, bye."

It has been said that when someone loses the use of some or one of his senses, other senses are strengthened to make up for the loss. Such was the case with James. He could hear a pin drop a hundred feet away. James heard the old rattletrap before it even got to the house. When it pulled up in front, he stopped what he was doing to see what could make such a "ruckus."

The ancient, green pickup truck door groaned with old age as it opened and a cracked and worn leather work boot stepped out onto the gravel. The old door complained again as it was forced to close against its will. Fran made it to the front door just as he was about to knock.

"Excuse me, mam," the old man said as he removed his hat. "I'm really sorry to bother you."

"That's okay," said Fran. She felt sorry for him as he humbly stood there turning his hat in his hands. But she really didn't feel like having to deal with a beggar, especially today of all days. "What can I do for you?"

The old man looked Fran over. He kind of felt sorry for her. She looked tired and had dark, puffy circles under her eyes as if she hadn't slept in weeks.

"Please don't let her say, no," he thought to himself.

"Well you see mam, I heard you need a little carpentering done."

"Well yes, we may but uh, my husband is not

home, and I don't know if uh---. "Boy," thought Fran, "I can't believe I just told him that Jim is not home. How stupid can I be? I don't even know this guy!"

"I understand mam, if you don't want me to do it," he said.

"No, no that's not it at all," replied Fran.

"Well, I know that I'm getting on in years and all and I may not be much to look at."

Fran, on the other hand, was thinking how distinguished the man looked, a little thin, but he had such beautiful silver hair and his eyes were so blue. When you looked deep into them, you could see warmth and compassion. "No," thought Fran, "it was more of a look of love or maybe all three rolled up into one."

"Why don't you wait, and my husband will be back shortly," said Fran.

"Exactly what kind of work do you need done, mam?"

"Well, it's this door."

"Looks like a fine door to me, mam."

"No, you don't understand. It's my son; he's a cripple. I mean he's in a wheelchair. You see his chair won't fit through the door."

"I see, and you need a larger door installed."

"That's right," said Fran. "The rest of the house has been remodeled already. Everything has been completed except the front door. Our son was just recently injured so we had to spend a great deal of time at the hospital. There just wasn't any way we could leave the house unlocked when we were not here. Have you ever done this before? I mean have you ever changed a door like this?"

The old timer scratched his silvery head and thought for a moment. "No, I can't say that I have, but I've been carpentering all my life. I'd sure like a try at it if you'll let me."

"I'm so sorry I haven't introduced myself. I've had kind of a bad day. I'm Fran Whitman," she said as she extended her hand.

"Yes, I know."

"You do?"

"Uh, yes, remember someone gave me your name about the job."

"Oh, yeah that's right."

"It's so nice to meet you Mrs. Whitman, I'm Gabe Michaels, father, grandfather, retiree, and jack of all trades. "What happened here?" asked Gabe, as he peered around Fran's shoulder.

Fran had forgotten all about the catastrophe that lay behind her. "Oh, I'm so embarrassed," she said, "I'm afraid it's James, our son."

"He did all this?"

"Yes," she said. "I don't know what we're going to do with him." Then she remembered that she was talking to a total stranger. Why was she telling him all this personal stuff? It was more like he was an old friend or her grandfather rather than a stranger. For some strange reason Fran just felt comfortable, at home with Gabe.

Before she realized it, Gabe had stooped down just inside the door and was just setting up an overturned flower stand. Gently he packed the soil back around the delicate roots of one of James' many victims.

"Oh, you don't have to do that," said Fran.

"I don't mind. I don't have anything better to do than just stand here. You don't mind, do you?" He was already inside the door and was retrieving a stack of scattered magazines.

"Uh, no I guess not." Fran felt a little funny having a stranger in her home. But he was just an old man. What harm could he do? Besides, James was here and the front door was open. He certainly appeared harmless. "Oh, no, James is here," she thought to herself. "I hope he doesn't make a scene. What if he doesn't like Gabe?"

Jim and Fran had never met Gabe that they remembered. Gabe had asked the police not to release his name to anyone. The day after the accident, the newspaper told of the tragedy and of the heroic efforts of inspector Johnson in finding and saving the family. No mention was ever made of how the police were notified or of the intricate details of the rescue. Gabe told the police that he was just doing what had to be done. Gabe said, "My mama and daddy have been gone for over twenty-five years, but there were two things they told me to always do. Always do what is right and always help someone who is not in a position to help themselves, especially little children, old folk, and ladies. So really, I was just doing what I was told to do. 'Nothin' special about that. I just don't want any publicity out of all this, so please don't use my name on anything that is to be released to the public." And with that he left the police station and never returned.

Jim pulled the old car into the drive and parked behind the antiquated pickup. Not recognizing the vehicle and seeing the front door wide open, he sprinted for the doorway. Not seeing Gabe down on the floor, Jim rushed right into him. Gabe had his back turned to the door as he picked up the last pile of dirt from another flower pot. Upon hearing the thundering hoofbeats, Gabe turned and ducked as Jim made an attempt to leap over him. Jim almost made it too, but his right foot caught in the lining of Gabe's tan windbreaker.

Jim lost his balance, went flailing and tripping

into the living room wall and then collapsed onto the hardwood floor. Laughter could be heard coming from the back of the house as James backed his wheelchair, slowly retreating into his lair. He had rolled out just far enough to see the stranger and what he was doing. Silently he had been eavesdropping on his mother and Gabe's conversation. James couldn't have asked for a better performance than he had just witnessed. He laughed until it hurt.

"James!" his dad yelled. He closed his door, but muffled laughter could still be heard coming down the hallway.

"Mr. Whitman, are you ok?" said Gabe.

"Oh, um, fine I think." Jim stood up and brushed himself off. Fran came rushing back into the room to see what had happened. "Jim, are you ok?"

"Yeah, I'm all right, I guess."

"What happened?"

"Well, I saw the strange vehicle in the drive and the open door, and I guess I was just worried about you. I ran through the door and didn't see him, this gentleman here, and well, you know the rest."

"I'm sorry Mr. Michaels; this is my husband Jim. Are you ok, Mr. Michaels?"

"Yes, I'm fine. You've might say we've already met. Just call me Gabe, Mr. Whitman, just like the rest of my friends.

"You know Gabe, you really do look familiar," said Jim looking quizzically at the old man.

"Are you trying to tell me that we've bumped into each other before? I don't think so! I believe I would have certainly remembered an experience like that."

All three started snickering, and as Fran looked at both of them sprawled out on the floor, they all three burst into laughter. It was a deep kind of let-loose sort of laugh that doesn't matter who's looking or what's happening. It was the healing kind of laugh that permeates your very soul.

James listened quietly until the laughter was reduced to a chuckle. Carefully, he leaned toward the door trying to hear anything else that could be heard.

"Mr. Michaels wants to work on the door for us."

"Oh really," said Jim. I was going to get that done later, but I guess now is as good a time as any. How much do you charge?"

"Don't worry about that, I promise not to break you."

"Do you charge by the hour or the job?"

"Well I'll tell you what, since you insist on getting a price, how does a hundred dollars or less sound to you? Of course, you provide all the materials."

"Uh, yeah, that sounds more than fair." In the back of his mind, though, Jim was thinking about that "or less" phrase. "Sure," he thought, "I've dealt with carpenters before."

"Yeah, but you've never dealt with me before."

Jim was shocked back into reality by Gabe's words.

"What, what did you say?"

"I said, I know you haven't seen my work or dealt with me before, but I promise if you're not happy, there will be no charge."

"Well, when can you start?"

"How about right now?"

"Now?"

"Well, yes, I'll give you the measurements, and you can go and pick out a door and have it delivered. Also go ahead and pick out the trim that you want to go around it. Might as well go ahead and pick up a pretty brass door knocker and kick plate while you're at it. And don't get anything cheap. I want my work to look top notch."

"Sure," thought Jim, "but how many notches is this going to take out of my wallet?" Jim thought to himself. "Anything else?" asked Jim.

"Well since you brought it up, let me make you a list."

After an extensive list was completed, Fran said, "You better hurry up Jim, or the hardware will be closed."

"If you think I'm going without you, you're crazy," said Jim. "I'm not picking out a door by myself. Do you remember the three sinks we sent back before you found one that you liked?"

"Well then, we will have to wait until we can get someone to stay with James," said Fran.

"Why don't you just take him with you," said Gabe looking back over his shoulder as he continued to work.

"We would like to, we really would," said Jim. Fran gave Jim the look that told him he had already said too much. But Jim continued explaining. "It's just that anywhere we've tried to take him, he always embarrasses people."

"What do you mean?" said Gabe as he stopped work to give his full attention.

"Three weeks ago, for example, we tried to take him to the mall. A young mother came by holding her little girl's hand, and you know how curious children are. The little girl never said anything. She just kept turning around and looking back at James in his wheelchair. James yelled at her, "What are you looking at, you little brat?" The little girl burst into tears. Her mother wasn't very happy either, to say the least. Can you imagine what that little girl will probably think about people in wheelchairs the rest of her life."

"Yeah, I kind of see what you mean. I tell you what, you see to whatever James needs and I'll stay here until you get back. You won't be gone more than an hour or so anyway, will you?"

"No, we shouldn't, but I don't know," said Jim.

"Listen, your boy will be fine, I promise. If you're concerned about me, I'll be glad to give you some references that you can call right now."

"No, that won't be necessary. I'm sure you're a fine person," said Fran.

"Well just the same, if you change your mind you can call my preacher; his name is Raylan Smith. I've done work for his sister Rayleigh Smith and their cousin Emeline Perkins. I'm sure any of them will be glad to talk to you, and can give you some other references as well."

"No, I'm sure that won't be necessary but thanks anyway. What do you say Fran?"

"I don't know, I guess so. Let me go back and see James and explain to him what's going on."

Fran returned in about five minutes and said, "All right, I'm ready. Mr. Michaels, we'll---" Gabe cleared his throat loudly indicating that he wasn't Mr. Michaels.

"Excuse me, I mean Gabe, we'll be back in about an hour or less. We will be at Andy's Hardware if you need us. Here is the number on the pad beside the telephone. I also left the number where our daughter can be reached.

"Now Mrs. Whitman, you just don't worry; everything will be fine, I promise; everything will be all right."

"Ok, I know, I'm just being a mother. James will just stay in his room until we return; he won't need a thing. We'll try to hurry."

"Now Mrs. Whitman, you and the mister just take your time. Everything will be just fine here."

Fran wished that could be true, but she had her doubts. She remembered the earlier events of the day. Finally, Jim and Fran backed out of the drive and headed toward town. When they got to the end of the street, Jim said, "There is a pay phone in front of the hardware. When we get there, we need to just check to be sure. It won't hurt and we'll feel better about it."

After arriving and after about a minute of searching the phone book for and through the S's Fran said, "Jim, there is no Raylan Smith listed in here."

"What!" said Jim.

"Wait a minute; here's an R. Smith; this must be the one."

Raylan Smith answered the telephone on the second ring. "Hello, this is Raylan, how can I help you?"

"Mr. Smith, this is Jim Whitman, I'm kind of new in town and I need a little advice."

"Sure Jim, what can I do for you?"

"I need a little work done around the house, and this afternoon this fellow showed up offering to do the work."

"Was it Gabe Michaels?"

"As a matter of fact, it was; how did you know?"

"Gabe just has a kind of sixth sense about showing up where he is needed. I'll tell you, he's the salt of the earth. I'd trust him with the last cent I own. You won't find a better man anywhere."

"Thanks a lot, I think you have already answered my question."

"Nothing is wrong with Gabe is there?" quizzed Pastor Smith.

"No, no, he's fine."

"Just keep an eye on him and don't let him over do it. You know he is getting on up in years."

"Sure, we'll be glad to and thanks for everything. Oh, by the way, please don't tell Gabe that I called."

"I won't, and if I can be of any more help, please feel free to call me. Are you by any chance the Whitman family that had the bad accident several months ago?"

"Actually, we are," said Jim.

"I was so sorry to hear about it and so sorry to hear about your son's injuries. If our church can be of service or again, if I can help any way please don't hesitate to call.

"Thanks, I may just take you up on that; thanks again, goodbye."

They just stood in silence for a moment; then Jim spoke up. "The minister spoke very highly of Gabe."

"So, we don't have anything to worry about?"

"According to the pastor, nothing at all, he said they don't come any better than Gabe."

"Good, that makes me feel a lot better."

Jim Took Fran's hand in his and they slowly strolled toward the hardware. For the first time in a long time they felt at peace knowing that they had time together without any responsibilities.

Gabe had made several trips out to his old

pickup to get the tools that he would need. His carpentry skills had been refined to that of a surgeon. He could take anything apart, fix it, and replace it with no signs of his ever having been there. The instruments he used were saws, chisels, hammers, files, and a multitude of various and sundry other devices for specialized surgery. His father had taught him many of the skills that he had picked up during his seventy years of carpentering. The rest he had learned by watching other carpenters, by examining their work, and by trial and error. All told his skills amounted to a doctor of carpentry. When he finished a job, people would always brag and boast about his excellent work.

Gabe even had a special way of making flaws in wood grain or knots look as if they were planned to be there to enhance his masterpiece. When he fixed something, it stayed fixed. He was considered a perfectionist in everyone's eyes but his own. Someone once commented that his work was perfect, never a mistake. Without hesitation he said, "Oh no, I have created many flaws. It's just that I can blend them in or cover them up. However, I do know a carpenter that is perfect; He doesn't make mistakes. He taught me more about life than He did about woodworking. He is the only builder that I know who can take a catastrophe and make something beautiful out of it; whether it's a bad situation or someone's wrecked life." Usually, he would share the story of his life and how this carpenter had made something complete out of a life that was empty before."

On one of his many trips out to the truck Gabe noticed, when he returned, a pair of toes and two foot-rest barely protruding through a doorway down the hall. When he set his tools down beside the door, he also noticed that the subtle noise that he made caused the perpetrator to slip quietly back into the shadows.

Whenever he started a new job, Gabe would always lay his tools on a rug, mat, or something in order not to create more damage than necessary. He didn't repair a cabinet and then leave scratch marks all over the floor. When he finished a job, it was complete, fixed, and finished. Usually, he would sweep or vacuum and if necessary, dust the area where he had worked.

His love for woodworking was only exceeded by his love for people. He had a great respect for others and their property. Because of this special love and respect he had for others, he also expected the same in return. Though he never verbalized or asked for it, it was as though his soul, his very countenance demanded respect. Gabe didn't have a chip on his shoulder or a holier-than-thou attitude. On the contrary, he was very meek and lowly. He would never strut around with his head in the clouds or put on airs as if he were someone special. He had a quiet and dignified disposition that everyone learned to respect within minutes of meeting him.

As he began pondering the task before him and what was needed to complete it, he allowed his mind to drift. He thought about James and how he looked when he had found him beside the little, rippling stream four months ago. From the talk he heard around the community he learned that in many ways James had made tremendous progress. At the same time, he had also heard other horror stories. Some said that James had seemed to slip back into the character of an animal, somewhat less than human. He had even heard the term "demonic" used as a description. Gabe pondered the job ahead. He wasn't there to repair a door; he was there to repair a boy. Gabe wondered if he was once again up to the challenge and whether he could really make a difference.

For a time, he reflected on other great challenges that had faced him through his lifetime. He thought about the three boys back several years ago who had taken it upon themselves to release their adolescent frustrations upon his old pickup truck. The three boys would have been considered losers by most people. They were flunkies in school who brought the streets into the classroom and usually spent a great deal of time in the school office or suspended from school. In the afternoons they would drift around town causing disturbances everywhere they went. They were not difficult to spot with their long hair and ragged clothes. They usually left a trail to follow as they meandered throughout the town. The sidewalks and street signs always lent themselves as good targets for shattering glass bottles and for spray painting if they managed to steal a can of spray paint.

When the boys chose Gabe as a target, they never realized they had sealed their own fate.

CHAPTER XIII

E ventually the three hoodlums began to cruise through Gabe's neighborhood. They were testing the waters, searching out their next hapless victim. At first, they would just walk by his yard and make smart remarks about his old pickup. They would say things like, "Hey mister, nice truck. Can I borrow it for my date Saturday night?" Then they would saunter on down the street with heckling laughter in their wake; the kind that makes people feel degraded and low. After a few days they graduated to water ballooning him as he drove his truck down the street.

They would hide in the woods and let him have it as he slowed to turn in his driveway when he least expected it. Then they would run away, once again splitting their sides with laughter. A week later they graduated to sticks and mud-dirt bombs. When small stones began hitting his door and tailgate, Gabe thought to himself, "Enough is enough. I'll put a stop to this once and for all."

Most people would have gone to the boys' parents or maybe even called the police. Gabe never called the police or even acted like his feathers were ruffled. From the ancient well of wisdom he drew from, he prayed that he would find an answer.

Then one day the answer hit him just as a dirt bomb exploded against his window. As the boys turned to run, Gabe rolled down his window and tossed all the change he had, out onto the pavement. He continued to drive as quarters, nickels, and dimes danced and rolled across the asphalt.

It was as if the dinner bell had rung and stopped the boys dead in their tracks. Since the truck hadn't stopped, they spun and headed back up the road pushing and shoving as they went. Each wanted to be first to grab the largest silver coins. It was a perfect picture of how the boys had degenerated into beings full of greed and selfishness. They proved they would turn on even a friend for just a few pieces of silver.

All three boys were about to come to blows when they suddenly froze. No one said a word. They had all felt the same thing, like that funny feeling you get when you slip a cookie out of the cookie jar. You don't think anyone is around, yet you have to turn around because you feel like someone is watching you.

The boys stopped and slowly turned around. Sure enough, the old man was standing there right behind them just staring and smiling. Instinct told them to flee, but because they were the tough guys, they stood their ground. After all, he was just one old man anyway. They were humiliated to think that an old man like he could slip up on them. If he were looking for a fight, he had come to the right place.

The oldest and toughest of the three took a step forward. He had an image to maintain. The two younger boys glanced at each other pondering what terrible tragedy their friend was about to invoke on the old man.

Glancing over his shoulder to make sure his reinforcements were watching and admiring him, the oldest boy began his presentation. "So what's your problem, old man? Hum, you must have forgot your medicine. Well you came to the right doctor. When I get through with you, you'll be in a home where you belong 'gummin' grits."

Gabe didn't say a word for a long time. He let the silence speak for him and work its own kind of magic. Inside he was doing a lot of talking to himself. He was calming himself down and gathering strength. When he finally did speak, it was not in wrath or anger. He didn't point a threatening finger or curse at them. Instead he spoke softly and slowly as he gave the boys their first dose of medicine.

"What's the matter old man, cat got your tongue?"

"I need you fellas to do me a favor," Gabe said. The boys looked at each other and started laughing and mocking him.

"He wants us to do him a favor," repeated one of the younger boys in a high, squeaky voice. He was very proud of himself, acting tough and stretching his wings a little. They all laughed and pointed at Gabe again believing themselves to have scored another point.

Gabe began to smile just a little and a small chuckle escaped his aged and wrinkled face. This unsettled the boys and gave them a case of nervous feet and to begin to question each other with their eyes as if to say, "what do we do now?" Then the silence scored another point and regained control as they just stood and stared at each other. While the boys struggled with trying to prove who was the boss and who was in control, Gabe wrote and orchestrated the music of the final movement. Finally, after an immortal period of silence, Gabe spoke.

"You boys got any money?"

"Why old man, you got some you 'gonna' give us?"

"Yes, as a matter of fact, I do."

The boys just kind of stared at each other for a moment. Their power and control had momentarily been rocked by this left punch from Gabe.

"Oh, don't think I give away money for free," said Gabe. "I always expect something in return."

"So, there is a catch," chided the oldest boy as he crossed his arms.

"You see my old truck," said Gabe pointing down the road.

"Yeah, what about it?"

"Well it's not much, but it is all I have. It has dirt all over it because of your dirt bombs."

The boys grinned with pride recognizing that their handiwork had been acknowledged.

"Now I don't have any problem with you boys working on your pitching arm; maybe you'll make it all the way to the major leagues. Then you'll have plenty of money and can buy me a new truck."

The boys' smiles faded at the thought of doing something nice for someone else.

"Man, please, you can forget---"

Gabe butted in, "Now let me finish. Here's the deal. I don't mind water balloons, but the dirt, sticks, and rocks must stop right now. I'll give you the money to buy water balloons with."

Slowly he reached back and removed an old, cracked, brown leather wallet from his trousers. The boys all noticed the wallet trembling a little as he opened it and took out the only green bill inside it. The boys noticed the trembling but also realized it was not out of fear. Holding a five-dollar bill, Gabe continued to talk but occasionally moved his hand as he watched the boys' eyes as they followed the path of the bill.

"You see, the water balloons will help keep my truck clean and rinsed off, and so basically, I'll be paying you to wash my truck the easy way." "But," said Gabe pointing his finger at them, "It has to be done my way."

"And how's that?" said one of the boys.

"I'm not buying you balloons to bomb some woman with two kids in the car. You could cause an accident and maybe kill someone that way. Then not only you but I could also wind up in jail because I bought the balloons. Only me, understood?"

"Yeah, ok, only you. When do we start?"

"Hold on now, I'm not finished." The boys refolded their arms across their chest as they once again began shifting their weight from foot to foot and releasing a deep breath as if to say, "Get on with it."

"You may water balloon me on any day but Sunday."

"Why not Sunday, the youngest asked?"

"'Cause' he'll be dressed for church stupid, the

oldest yelled." He was proud to have thought of it. His mom and dad used to take him to church. That was, of course, before they began fighting a lot, stopped going to church and then later got divorced.

"Ok, let me get this straight. We can nail you any day but Sunday."

"Yes, that's right but only at 9:00. That's usually about the time I leave in the morning."

They readily agreed, not thinking that their summer vacation would be ending soon.

"That way, I'll be expecting it, and I won't have a wreck and get killed or kill someone else. I'll agree to give you five dollars a week for as long as you keep it up. So, I get my truck washed, you get to work on your throwing arm, and then everybody's happy. So, do we have an agreement at $5.00 a week?"

The boys turned and began murmuring among themselves. They knew the balloons cost only $1.00 which left $4.00 a week profit. That's $16.00 a month, and they didn't even have to work for it. On the contrary, they were going to get paid for water ballooning someone. This old coot was going to pay them to bomb him. This was almost too good to be true.

"Yeah, we'll do it! Hand over the money, old timer."

Gabe handed the money to the boys and triumphantly they marched away laughing and slapping each other on the back. He watched them walk away down the street bragging about how they had pulled one over on the old man. Gabe just stood there, quietly watching and smiled to himself.

Gabe was up early the next morning. He wanted to make sure that he was at his appointment at exactly 9:00. As he turned onto the street, he noticed that at one point on the road, the bushes appeared a little more dense than usual.

Sure enough, as he approached the wooded area there was a terrible war cry and out of the bushes popped three blood thirsty savages. All three drew back but waited until the oldest boy gave the order to fire. They each had a grocery bag full of the multicolored missiles.

Balloons came from every direction and the steel of Gabe's old truck rang and thudded as the projectiles found their mark. Gabe was the perfect actor. As the balloons hit his windshield and the windows in his truck, he threw his hands up and leaned away as if in a panic. The boys loved it and gave each other high fives each time a balloon found its mark.

The same scenario continued for three days. On the third morning Gabe waved at the boys as he slowly approached the target zone. All three waved back.

"Yep, everything is working right on schedule," Gabe mumbled to himself.

On the fourth morning, Professor Gabe decided that it was time for his students to take their first exam. As he turned down the street that morning, he noticed that his desperados no longer feared enough to hide. They were lined up along the side of the road waiting on their prey. Gabe had rolled both windows down on the old truck earlier that morning. As he neared them, he held his arm out the window and gave them a big wave and a thumbs up.

They would have waved back but couldn't because their arms cradled so many of the delicate weapons. However, as he approached, Gabe noticed a smile begin to grow on each boys' face. "Must have run out of grocery bags," he thought to himself as he saw all the balloons each was carrying.

"Well, here goes," he said aloud. "What's the worst that can happen, I'll get wet."

As Gabe approached, bombs once again began to fly, and his bunker took a real pounding. Everything happened just as Gabe had hoped it would. As he slowed to a stop, he decided to survey the damage. His truck was dripping with water, but not one single water balloon had flown through either window. Actually, none had come even close. There was not a single drop of water inside. "Yes, his students were coming along nicely," thought Gabe. He chuckled to himself thinking that they had passed the test with "flying colors."

The next morning Gabe had another treat in store for his young proteges. As he approached the boys, he held up his hand motioning for them to wait. The boys followed the instructions of their leader, and the safety was momentarily set on their firing arms. The truck had almost passed them when Gabe yelled, "Bombs away."

That's when the boys saw it. Gabe had painted and fastened a board with a large red bull's eye on the tailgate of his truck. The boys became almost giddy when they spied it. They let loose with a flurry of bombs as never before. The old truck took a terrible pounding but still stood solid like a mighty fortress of old.

The next day was Sunday, and Gabe went to church as scheduled. The boys kept the truce, and the battle ground fell silent the entire day. The young comrades sat at home moping about and in general were just plain miserable. As the day waned and the promise of a new day approached, the boys became more and more excited.

A strange thing began happening around town

during the days, weeks, and months ahead. Calls of complaints to the police dropped. There was far less graffiti painted on walls and signs. Cost of replacing damaged signs, broken windows, and other costly vandalism dropped dramatically. Police officers and city officials were left scratching their heads wondering what was going on around town. Little did they know that one old carpenter was busy rebuilding the lives of three young boys.

What the boys saw the next morning was a real shocker. Gabe's truck was not at home at the appointed hour. They began to wonder what was going on when they abruptly heard a distressing noise coming from up the street. It was Gabe's truck but it was coming from the opposite direction and headed toward his house. They cocked their weapons and released the safety but they were shocked at what they saw as the old truck rattled past. The bull's eye was still there, but it was ten times smaller. In order to score a hit, they really had to take their time and carefully aim.

Then Gabe did the unthinkable; he began to speed up and pull away before they could release even half of their missiles. It looked like the charge of the light brigade all over again. They began to charge and attack the old war horse following it right down the street. On and on they ran following, yelling, and catapulting their rainbow of bombs onto the target on the old truck, right into

DAVID PERKINS

enemy territory. Gabe turned into his driveway just as the last bomb found its mark.

The old truck rattled to a stop and then fought to stay alive as the ancient engine sputtered and then died. The young soldiers had stopped at the driveway entrance as if they believed it to be untouchable, holy ground.

Gabe waved them over, "Come here boys, I have something I want to give you."

The boys cautiously inched forward as if they were approaching the magnificent Wizard of Oz. Gabe extended his hand to each of the boys and gave them a firm handshake. Gabe's hands were rigidly firm and felt like shaking an oak limb. The character built into them had been placed there by years of hard, tough, backbreaking work.

"Consider your contract fulfilled gentlemen."

"What contract said one of the boys? We didn't sign any contract."

"Always remember this guys, A man's word is his bond," said Gabe.

"What do you mean by that?" the oldest said accusingly.

"A man is only as good as his promise," replied Gabe. "You want to be men, real men? Then you stand by your word and do everything you can to honor it. When a man shakes hands, that is his word to be honorable and to do everything in his power to honor his word. You don't have to have a written contract; your handshake is your contract."

"Wait here," Gabe said then turned and disappeared for a minute into the old white house. The guys all stopped to survey their surroundings. The paint on the old white, clapboard, wooden house had faded and begun to peel many years ago. The shrubbery, while greatly varied, had been given the freedom to express itself in natural growth. In general, the whole place had a very unkempt appearance. It was obvious to all three that the old timer must be pretty lazy. Even their own yards were kept better than this. Later they were to find that it was not Gabe who was at fault, but they who were poor at judging character.

Gabe was a harder worker than all of them put together. In truth, he had neglected himself and his property while looking after others. Most were widows who could not even afford to pay him. The majority of his income from jobs of this nature was given in thank you's and lemonade.

Finally, Gabe returned with three glasses of milk and some cookies.

"Sorry guys, but this is the best I can do."

The boys looked at each other as if this was some sort of a trick. After all, all three of them were now "veteran, street hardened drinkers." "Milk and cookies!" they thought. "Had this old coot stepped out of the middle ages?" One of the boys was about to laugh until the oldest elbowed him in the side.

Gabe extended the tray towards them, "Come on guys, eat up!"

"Could this be a way to get even for all they had done to him? Could the cookies or milk have something in them?" thought the boys as they quietly searched each other's eyes for affirmation.

John, the oldest, was the first to courageously step forward and receive the offering. Matt and Luke followed suit, and soon all three had downed all the milk and cookies.

"I'd offer you more boys but that's all I have.

"That's ok," said John, "It was um, it was good."

"Oh, I almost forgot, I believe it's pay-day. Here is the five bucks that I owe you."

John took the money but not as readily or greedily as he had the week before. He was not used to being nice, but he made a feeble attempt at it anyway.

"Tell, um, your wife that we uh, thought the cookies were good."

"I wish I could son, but my wife has been gone for many years."

"Oh," said John. "I didn't realize you were divorced."

"Didn't say I was," said Gabe. "No, me and Naomi were married for thirty-eight years, but she was killed by a drunk driver. She's been gone for almost ten years now," Gabe said with a sigh.

John, wanting to change the subject, noticed an old anvil sitting atop a stump over behind the house.

"Hey, that's one of those old things that blacksmiths used to use to beat horse shoes on, isn't it?"

"Yep," Gabe said. It's called an anvil and there is quite a story attached to that one.

CHAPTER XIV

Gabe spent the next hour telling the history of anvils, particularly his. It seems that his Great-Grandfather used to be a traveling smithy. He went from town to town and farm to farm repairing tools, shoeing horses and mules, and doing just about everything else that needed to be done.

"See that chipped place there on the back corner?" asked Gabe.

The boys nodded in response as they walked over to the anvil placing their hands on the cold iron and rubbing the broken corner with their fingers.

"When I was about ten years old, I tied a rope around it and pulled it up into a tree behind my brother's and my bedroom. One of my brothers was always pestering me so it was time for a little payback."

The boys began to smile just a little trying to picture in their minds what was coming next.

"I was careful to tie it off so it wouldn't fall on anyone. Later that night I slipped out and ---"

Gabe had to stop and chuckle to himself. As he looked at the boys, they were beginning to chuckle, too. Gabe realized they didn't even know what they were laughing at.

"Quietly, I raised the bedroom window and pulled in the rope that I had hidden under it after supper. We slept on bunk beds since there were so many of us. I had four brothers and two sisters."

Gabe was a true story teller. He went through all the motions as he told the story, relived it, and acted it out in front of his small audience.

"I waited until my brother was sound asleep and then I slipped the rope under the bracing boards of my brother's upper bunk and tied it off around the end of the mattress. Finally, everything was set. All that was needed to set the trap into motion was a gentle nudge of the anvil up in the tree.

Gabe paused for a moment.

"Well, what happened?" shouted the youngest boy, twisting his hands as he spoke.

"I knew my brother wouldn't be hurt because my bunk was right under his. I went back outside, climbed up on the door of the outhouse, and then climbed onto the roof."

"The out what?" questioned Matt.

"Don't be so stupid; it's the bathroom outside

DAVID PERKINS

in a shed!" announced Luke proudly.

Gabe gave him a nod of approval and a wink of the eye.

"I can still feel the peach switch on the seat of my pants," said Gabe.

"You got a 'beatin?'" questioned Matt.

"A 'beatin,' I got two! It wasn't really a 'beatin,' my daddy called them spankings, but whatever they were they left a lasting impression."

"Well, what did you get it for, what happened?"

"It, you mean them," said Gabe.

"I climbed back up in the tree, so proud of my ingenious plan. I untied the anvil and slid it over to the edge of the limb. For a moment I thought about tying it back up again and just forgetting the whole thing. Oh, how I wish I had! But I thought, 'I've gone this far, I might as well go all the way.' So, I began my count-down. 'Ten-Nine-Eight-Seven, Six, Five, Four, Three, Two, One, Blast Off!' Then I gave it a good, hard push. I turned to watch the window as the slack rope began to fly by. All of a sudden, the rope became tight, and I heard a mighty yell, echo from inside the bedroom. It was then that I realized why I was so hesitant to push the anvil off the limb. Something had been bothering me all along, but I didn't know what it was. It was at that point in my life that I learned to think

158

before I started to act. Do you know what happens when you force a three-and-a half foot mattress along with boards to match through a two-and-a half foot window?"

Gabe began to shake his head. "I'll tell you, it wasn't a pretty picture."

The boys began to howl. They were slapping each other on the back and laughing to the point of tears.

"My brother was certainly shaken up. One minute he was sleeping peacefully and the next, everything supporting him was snatched away and left him suspended in space, for a second anyway. He had trouble sleeping for a month. I finally had to give him the bottom bunk along with my mattress because he had developed a fear of falling. I, on the other hand, inherited the old twisted and mangled mattress that had made the trip through the window."

"Then what happened?" asked John.

"I hurried back into the house as fast as possible, but I was too late. I met my dad coming down the hall with a kerosene lamp. After checking on my brother and seeing the shattered window, he called me for a very serious conference. Believe it or not, I had to go outside in the dark and break my own switch off the old peach tree. I tell you the truth, we had the only one-sided peach tree in town. All the limbs on one side had been removed for disciplinary purposes. Well I got a good one that night and another one early the next morning. I knew it was too good to be true that I could actually get by that easy."

"Early the next morning I heard noises downstairs in the kitchen, so I knew my mom and dad were up. My dad always built a fire in the wood stove for my mama to do the cooking. Then I heard the screen door on the back-porch slam. I figured it must be my dad. I rolled over to catch a few more winks when I heard the screen door slam again. But this time it didn't sound natural. Instead of slamming shut, it was slammed forcefully back against the wall. Then I heard angry footsteps coming up the stairs. For the first time in my life, I was truly terrified of my dad."

"I ran to the window or to where the window used to be trying to find a means of escape."

Gabe started to chuckle once again and the guys knew a good part was coming up.

"I looked out the window and felt my blood drain all the way down to my toes. You see when I pushed the anvil out of the tree, I neglected the law."

"Which law is that?" asked Matt.

"The law of gravity! For you see just under the old oak tree was the outhouse. In you wildest dreams you cannot imagine what a seventy-five-pound anvil can do to the tin roof of an old outhouse after falling twenty-five feet."

The boys finally had to sit down after envisioning the outhouse exploding from the impact of the anvil.

"Needless to say, I regret ever taking that anvil up into that tree. Not only did I have to pay for the window, I had to fix that stinking outhouse, and got two 'switchings' on top of that."

"Yeah, this old anvil has a lot of memories. Some of them rather painful. And that's where that big nick came from in the corner. I guess it happened sometime between falling out of the tree and crashing all the way through the outhouse. I'm just glad nobody was in the outhouse. I may have been charged with murder!" The boys howled, holding their sides because they were hurting from laughing.

Finally, after several other stories about different things around the house, the boys moped off down the road and reluctantly headed for home.

The next morning Gabe found two five-dollar bills on his truck seat. He folded them gently and replaced them in his wallet. He made his rounds on schedule, but the boys were nowhere to be found. Gabe had made a deal, and he had always been known as a man of his word.

Later that same day he noticed the boys coming down the street. At different times they all cast glances toward the house as they passed and headed onward.

After a while Gabe saw them coming back down the street. This time they were walking a little slower and definitely straining to see whether he was anywhere around. Quietly Gabe eased out of the house. He started moving things around and straightening up the inside of the truck. He pretended that he happened to see them totally by accident.

"Hi, Guys," he called.

All three nonchalantly waved back, the cool wave.

"Come on over," Gabe yelled.

The boys walked so fast they almost broke into a run.

"Hey, I missed you guys this morning; where were you?"

"Uh," John spoke up, "we had some errands to run."

They talked for a while about the good old days and how things used to be. By the time they left, they knew what a carburetor was and how to adjust it, at least one on an old pickup anyway. As the boys started to leave, Gabe said. I'll be back out later; I 'gotta' try to clean this old girl up some. 'Gotta' doctor's appointment tomorrow in the big city. I'll see 'ya' later, 'yall' stop back by."

The three musketeers kind of dragged their feet as they left, which of course, didn't go unnoticed by Gabe. Gabe stayed in the house until he didn't hear the water running through the pipes in the house anymore. When he ventured outside a few minutes later, his garden hose was neatly stacked beside the house, and the old green truck was still dripping. As the final rinse began to slide off the old chrome bumper, the mid-days sun rays caught it just right. "Look at you old girl; you look like you just came out of the showroom."

The next morning Gabe left a letter thanking the boys and saying what a good job they had done beside his back door. As he drove down the street, he noticed the boys standing on the other side of a vacant lot. Before he even got close, he saw them smiling and waving. He waved back and yelled, "I'll see you after dinner. I left something for you beside the back door." He didn't worry anymore about their being around his house when he wasn't there. He had found a trust in them. More importantly, they had found trust in him.

No matter where they went or what happened to them. No matter what the world thought about them or how their parents treated them, one person believed in them, and that made all the difference in the world. As he drove down the street, Gabe watched his young cadets shrink in the rear-view mirror and said aloud, "Mission accomplished."

The boys' friendship continued to grow with Gabe, and later they even formed a club. Gabe had taught them some of his favorite Bible stories, and they chose one of his stories for their club name. The charter of their secret club listed them as "THE GOOD SAMARITANS." The four of them would try to spend one afternoon a week doing something extra nice for someone. They would rake yards, cut grass, sweep driveways and in general do anything that needed doing. They would always try to do it when the person was not home. They always left their business card which Gabe had printed for them. It was a simple card that just said, "THANKS," The Good Samaritans.

Gabe was the nearest thing they had to a real father until they graduated from high school and left for college. Every six-weeks during high school, each one of the boys would bring their report card for Gabe's approval. Any important decision they had to make was also ran by Gabe sometimes even years after they had left. They all were married and had families now of their own. Sadly, they had all moved away chasing their own dreams. All three turned out to be successful, but they never hesitated to give full credit to Gabe.

They always called or came by at Christmas or on his birthday. He was their hero. He would always assure them, though, that what made them happy and successful was always on the inside anyway. He had just helped them to find it. They all said that had it not been for Gabe, they would all have ended up in prison or dead. Once they had asked him why he did it, why he took out time for three hoodlums who would have just as soon robbed him as spoken to him? He answered that it wasn't himself but one who lived in his heart that allowed him to do what he did. Plus, he added, he didn't like having a dirty truck.

How long he had been day-dreaming and reflecting he didn't know. He sure had gotten bad about that lately. Gabe glanced down the hallway and saw James' wheelchair still protruding from the door. Gently he continued to pry the molding from around the doorway. He was very careful to not break it and to not make a mess. Sheetrock began to break off the molding and sprinkle onto everything around it. Gently he lifted one end of the sofa and slid it away from the wall all the while being cautious about scratching the floor beneath it. It took all his strength to budge it, but finally he prevailed, and it gently gave way to his urgings.

Softly he began to hum, but the hum was shortly transposed into a little song. He continued to sing softly, never missing a beat as he saw out of the corner of his eye the wheelchair silently slip out into the hallway behind him. He continued working around the door intentionally turning his back toward James. He knew what James was capable of; he had just spent thirty minutes cleaning up his handiwork. Steadily and silently the chair glided down the hallway. James was extra careful not to allow the rubber wheels to squeak on the wood floor as he gently made course changes. James moved cautiously and steadily toward his prey as a viper would slither from its hole in search of a victim. Closer and closer he came until he was right behind the old man.

CHAPTER XV

J ames stopped just short of Gabe, hoping that Gabe would step back and trip over him and the chair. He knew this would be a humbling experience for the old man. He would be so shocked and it would result in a stream of stammering apologies from the old timer.

He liked the power the chair gave him over people. He used to be embarrassed, but now he enjoyed watching the reactions that he got from people when they saw him in the chair for the first time. His chair had gone from a handicap to a throne. Now he was the king and the little people were just his puppets waiting to do their little dance as he commanded. He knew just what to say or do to make people cry or laugh or to do whatever he bid them to do.

This old man was to become his next victim. Little did he know that the roles had been reversed and that now he was the prey and the old man the hunter. James was so caught off guard by Gabe that he didn't have time to do anything but react.

Gabe never turned around. Sticking his hand out behind him, he just placed his order.

"James, hand me the screwdriver beside my toolbox. I need it now. I haven't got all day, hurry up!"

The old man had said it so forcefully and with such command that before James realized it, he was stretching, grasping, and then handing Gabe the screwdriver.

"Not that way!" said Gabe as James thrust the screwdriver with the pointed end toward Gabe. "You always pass a tool with the blunt end or handle toward the other person."

Gabe had still not turned around. James was bewildered, he didn't realize that Gabe was watching his reflection in the window. After James turned the screwdriver around the correct way, Gabe turned just enough for James to see his face and Gabe reached a wrinkled hand out for the screwdriver.

"Thanks," Gabe said as he returned his attention to his work. Not another word was said. James turned and retreated into the kitchen to regroup.

"Well, he might have gotten the best of me this time," James thought, "but he won't do it again. I'll show him!"

James was furious. His face grew red and his breathing became rapid and shallow as he seethed, stewing in his anger. Then another battle plan began to form in his mind, a very diabolical plan. James spun his chair to initiate phase one of his latest plan, but his chair struck something solid, something immovable.

Gabe's boot and leg had blocked the chair just short of a full turn. The old man had been standing right there watching him the whole time.

"Oh, I'm sorry, James, I didn't mean to get in your way. I need something to drink. May I get some water?"

James, once again caught off-guard, was almost speechless.

"Yeah, uh yeah, I guess that's ok."

Gabe walked over to the sink and took a clean glass from the drain. He filled it with tap water and then drained it. James watched, somewhat fascinated, as his Adam's Apple bobbed up and down in the old man's brown, leathery throat.

"Well, back to work. Thanks for the water."

Gabe turned and headed back toward the living room. As he approached James, he showed no indication of going around him, and James found himself back-peddling to keep from getting run over. Was it his imagination or did he notice a little smirk on the old man's face as he strode past?

"That was it," thought James. At first, he had found the old man somewhat fascinating but now, "the gauntlet had been thrown down and the die cast." "There was no turning back now."

"Very well," thought James. "I'm not afraid of an old man. I'll teach him a thing or two."

Gabe went back to his work in the living room, leaving James alone, sulking in the kitchen. Quietly James once again approached his target. Gabe knew James was malicious, but what James proceeded to do was something even Gabe could not foresee nor was he ready mentally to deal with.

Slithering forward, James rolled closer and closer to the old man. Gabe, although advanced in years, still had pretty good hearing. He heard the sound as James' hands rubbed the tops of the wheels of the wheelchair as he crept across the room. He heard the wheels as they slightly gripped the beautiful hardwood floor and moved ever closer. Onward and onward they came until there was only silence. James had arrived and was ready to pounce.

Gabe had put his tool box on a rubber mat on the coffee table. He always carried the little thin mat with him to set his tools on so nothing would get scratched. Ever so slowly James slid one end of the heavy tool box off the edge of the table so that he could slip his fingers under it. Now it was James with the smirk across his face.

With all his might, James thrust the end of the

box into the air, flipping it end over end. The box and all its contents hit the floor with a mighty crash. Tools bounced and slid across the floor like water on a hot griddle.

Gabe didn't jump or even flinch when the tools fell and fanned out across the hardwood floor. Slowly turning, his countenance did begin to transform, to change. Then he saw the deep gouge cut into the once beautiful hardwood oak flooring. There weren't many things that could cause Gabe to lose his temper. He was usually quiet and reserved. If it could be said that Gabe Michaels had a fault though, it would be his quick temper. Intentional waste, needless destruction, cruelty to a child, a lady, an old person, or even an animal could send him into orbit. It seemed to be this fault, which had a way of flaring up occasionally that caused him the greatest humility. The fuel had been spread; all Gabe needed was a spark to set him off and James ignited it.

"You Moron!" James yelled. "Look what you did."

Not only had James done it, but he was also going to blame it on Gabe.

Slowly a storm began to brew deep down inside Gabe's innermost being. It grew and spread throughout his extremities. His fingers flexed as he remained crouching on the floor. Veins began to swell under his wrinkled forehead and color began to pulsate across his face. The man that once held the countenance of an angel now was transformed into a kind of primordial beast that somehow breached the eons of time to revenge its demise. Gabe spun to face James. The "I gotcha" smirk suddenly vanished from James' face to be replaced with pure, unadulterated fear. James thought he could literally see the eyes that had once been sky blue bulging and pulsating in their sockets. It was as if consuming flames were about to burst forth and incinerate James in a great blaze.

"I'm sorry, I'm sorry, I'm sorry!" James found himself stammering helplessly. He was all alone with this man, this stranger. "What was he about to do to him?" James thought as he shriveled back into his chair.

Gabe lunged for James's chair as James frantically tried to force the wheels backward. Too late. Gabe's hand had locked onto one of the wheels. The chair froze motionless and time stopped. The old, World War ll drill sergeant that Gabe had held at bay for so many years suddenly re-emerged. Gabe grabbed a fistful of James' shirt and almost lifted him out of the chair as he drew him closer in. James opened his mouth to scream, but the words wouldn't come. His muscles felt like water; his jaw moved up and down, but only raspy breaths escaped. James didn't know it yet but he was beginning to realize, too late, that he had met his match.

CHAPTER XVI

With noses all but touching, James stared into the burning blue eyes that held him captive. "How could this old man do this? He didn't look that strong, and he was old, too. Where did he get such strength? Could he be a murderer or something? Why did his parents leave him alone with a man like this?" A thousand questions flooded James' mind all at once.

"Hey, boy," Gabe said, stressing the word "boy." "Who do you think you are?" he yelled. "I'm nobody, nobody sir, I'm sor----", Gabe cut him off, "Oh no you don't. Don't you come in here and try to say you're sorry for something you did on purpose. And about you accusing me of coming here and doing this, don't you even think about saying I did this!" "No sir, no sir, I wouldn't ever say that!" James stammered as he shook his head no.

James looked away from the bulging eyes.

"Look at me when I'm talking to you, boy!"

James' eyes returned to the unblinking eyes of the old man who now appeared forty years younger.

"Do you really think you can come in here and trash your own house? I've already cleaned it up one time, but it was the last time. If you do it again, I'll clean it up with your face! Do you understand me?"

James frantically nodded his head.

"Answer me when you talk to me, boy!"

"Yes, sir," James squeaked.

"What?" said Gabe, still yelling. "Speak up when you talk to me. I didn't mumble to you, and you don't mumble to me. Do you understand that?"

"Yes, sir!" James yelled back.

"You're not going to mess up this house again are you, boy?"

"No, sir!"

"And you're going to pick up my tools that you threw on the floor. Isn't that right Mr. Whitman?"

"Yes, sir" James responded.

Gabe took a deep breath trying to calm himself down. Releasing his grip, Gabe allowed James to settle back in his chair.

"If you take care of your tools, son, your tools will take care of you. That's what my dad used to tell me. Why I've never, I've never thrown my tools down like that." Gabe stood erect panning the

DAVID PERKINS

menagerie of tools scattered about the floor.

After an eternity of quiet when neither of them moved, Gabe spoke first, "Well, get at it then boy."

James looked down at the vast multitude and variety of tools scattered all over the floor. A little smile escaped his lips as he turned to Gabe who had taken a step back.

"I can't reach them," James responded. Then he leaned back in his chair with a disrespectful sigh, crossed his arms and presented an arrogant smile.

James had fired the last shot but he didn't realize what little impact his words had actually made. They had just detonated on the surface doing no damage within.

"Well," said Gabe. "If the work can't come to you, then I guess you'll have to go to the work."

Gabe took one step back toward the chair and James' smart-aleck smile disappeared. With lightning speed, Gabe grabbed both wheels and engaged the locks.

"Common boy, you're only as much of a cripple as you make yourself out to be."

"Who are you calling a -----"

James' words were lost in the confusion as Gabe grabbed him under his arms and lifted him from the chair. He firmly but gently laid him on the floor among the array of tools.

176

Gabe turned around and returned immediately to his work without saying another word. James was fuming at first. As he began to pick up the tools, he began to notice how strange and different they were. There were tools of all shapes and sizes, most he'd never seen before. Then again many were like hammers, yet they were still very different and yet very similar. Some hammers were big and some small. Some had claws on their heads while others had a spike or a chisel on the back of their heads. Two or three times he started to ask questions about the tools, but because of his pride he kept quiet.

As usual, Gabe was taking all this in but had not said a word. In reality, he was more furious with himself than with James for letting his temper get the best of him. Yet, something good could come of his outburst. He left James to himself, to let the fruit ripen. When it was mature and ripe, Gabe would know and he would harvest the fruit and bring James into the fold.

As he continued steadily working and watching James out of the corner of his eye examining the tools with the inquisitive nature of a jeweler; Gabe tried to remember the last time he had lost his temper that badly. He thought but for a moment and then remembered a time he almost got into some really serious trouble.

Gabe had gone to visit family in Chicago. The

previous day the news media had announced that a group planned to express its Freedom of Speech by burning an American Flag in downtown Chicago. Naturally the announcement drew a large crowd. Gabe and his family, knowing nothing of the planned demonstration, noticed the crowd as they strolled down Michigan Avenue the following day. Gabe, hearing a loud speaker and seeing an American Flag held high, figured it must be some kind of a patriotic demonstration. Being a veteran, he never passed up an opportunity to let his true allegiance be known.

Casually he strolled over and immediately was concerned by the appearance and the foul language of the crowd. They didn't appear to be your regular dyed-in-the-wool true-blue Americans. As he got closer, he could hear anti-American slurs and a lot more profanity being used. When he was within eight feet, he saw someone spit on the flag and then curse it and all the baby killing soldiers who loved it.

Gabe saw red. Not only the red of the stripes on the flag, but the same red he saw on the bodies of his friends and his brothers as the blood slowly drained from their wounded and dead bodies and seeped into the sand on the battlefields and on the beaches. As he reached for the demonstrator, he saw something even more terrifying. Another anti-war demonstrator had a plastic lighter which he fired up and stretched toward the corner of the flag.

Gabe was never one to seek the spotlight or try to be a celebrity. His friends had died for the Freedom of Speech that allowed these demonstrators to protest. They hadn't died though, so that these people could burn the very symbol that gave them this freedom.

However, the next day he was featured on the front page of the newspaper. The 5x7 picture depicted an old "war horse" soldier parading down Michigan Avenue with an American Flag on a six-foot pole.

In the foreground, fuzzy but visible, were three long haired war protestors lying on the ground nursing a multitude of bumps and bruises. The caption under the picture read, "And his response was, 'No Sir, Not Today You Won't!'" Gabe smiled as he thought of that same old flag now hanging proudly on the wall under his garage.

The jingling of tools brought the world back into focus. Gabe had been casually watching James, and even though he was slow, he was putting the tools back into the tool box. It was time for the first test. "James, hand me a small pry bar if you don't mind."

For an instant, but only for an instant, James considered balking at the request.

"What's a pry bar?"

"It's the crooked little flat bar about three feet over to your right." Gabe knew the easiest thing to do would be to just go and get it himself. James would have to drag himself over to the pry bar and then turn around and drag himself back to Gabe. James paused to contemplate the distance, then looked back at Gabe.

Gabe could see the questioning and doubt beginning to spread across James' face. He needed a little push.

Gabe, raising his voice ever so slightly said, "What's the matter; is it too tough for you?"

James expression of doubt quickly switched to one of determination and an, "I'll show you look."

James defensively spun around back in the direction of the pry bar. He slapped his arm down on the brightly varnished floor and then began to pull. Slowly the rest of his body heeded the call to service. Inch by inch he reached and stretched out for his goal. Again, and again his hands slapped the floor. He groaned and moaned as he used muscles which all but refused to return to service.

Gabe showed no emotion on the outside; he just continued working. On the inside, however, he was cheering wildly.

When James finally reached the bar, he almost

held it over his head and shouted. A look of, "I showed you didn't I," glowed across his face.

"Still 'waitin' on that bar," said Gabe.

James arm slapped the floor hard as he grunted and began his return trip.

Gabe said, "Hey, son," James stopped in mid grunt and looked up. "Be careful and don't scratch the floor," said Gabe.

A look of contempt grew on James' face, and he pushed even harder to reach the old man. He fully intended to drop the heavy pry bar across the old man's toes when he got there. Of course, Gabe was ready for anything. He had always said that "big old fish didn't get big and old by being stupid. You have to be on your toes all the time."

As James neared the blind side of his victim, he raised the bar like a cobra preparing to strike. Just as James was about to slam the bar down, Gabe spun and grabbed him by the wrist. Quickly Gabe removed the bar from his hand. With the other hand he grabbed James' hand and gave him a firm handshake worthy of a man and said, "Congratulations." Just as quickly, Gabe laid the tool down, and then grabbed James and replaced him on his throne.

"Might as well have a seat," said Gabe.

The tools left on the floor were mostly ones

that he would need shortly, so he didn't ask James to finish picking them up. Gabe stopped working for a minute and looked at the wounded floor. James also diverted his attention to the floor when he saw Gabe staring at the deep gash.

"Pretty deep cut, isn't it?" Gabe said, speaking with deep emotion in his voice.

James just sat without speaking yet he noted the deep concern and even sorrow in Gabe's voice. Gabe reached down, gently caressing the deep wound as if the floor were a wounded lamb.

"Your mom and dad trusted me to take care of things while they were gone and this is what they get for trusting me," said Gabe. For the first time the pride James felt in manipulating and destroying was not so great. He even felt a little sorry that the old man may get blamed for what he himself had done. James wasn't sure but he thought he may even see some extra moisture in the old man's eyes.

First, Gabe took a piece of coarse sandpaper and smoothed out the ragged splinters. Then he used medium sandpaper to work the rough edges down. Gabe handed the sandpaper to James between sandings for him to hold. He noted how James rubbed the paper with his fingers to feel the difference between the two different grades of paper.

"What are you doing?" asked James.

"First, I have to get out all the broken pieces.

I'm going to put in a patch, and when we're finished, it should be hard to tell the patch from the real floor."

"Why didn't you sand it all the way down?" said James.

"The patch has to have something to hold on to. If I sanded it smooth like a bowl, the patch may pop right out. Leaving the floor a little rough will give the patch some good handles. Be right back."

Gabe stood up and marched out the door. James looked at the tool box perched back on the coffee table, but for some reason he no longer had the urge to dump it. He could hear the old truck doors groaning and moaning as Gabe searched for the special ingredients he needed. Finally, Gabe reappeared in the front door. He walked in with a can of wood putty, several cans of stain, an old spoon, and an old cereal bowl.

Gabe took the old stained, cereal bowl and filled it about half full with wood putty. To this he added a little of one stain, then more from another can and another. He looked like a chemist concocting some new and dangerous substance. Gradually he added stain to the putty until it was just the right color and consistency. James was, mesmerized. Finally, Gabe announced, "That's it."

James looked at the putty and said, "It's too dark."

"It will lighten as it dries, smarty pants," Gabe chuckled.

Even James had the faintest hint of a smile.

Meticulously, Gabe packed every small cut and crevice until it was over filled and worked the putty like dough until all the air pockets were worked out.

James, the 'expert carpenter and know it all' spoke up, " 'Ya' got too much in it; it's humped up over the floor."

"Sometimes, son, you can't look at the whole of something or someone. You must look at all the parts. Did you learn in science how much of your body is made of water?"

"About three-fourths, I believe."

"That's exactly right, and if you took all that water out, what would happen to you?"

"I'd die of course!"

"I mean, what would happen to the solid part of your body?"

"It would get smaller or shrink, I guess, because all the water would be gone."

"Now you tell me what you think will happen to the putty?"

"Well, I guess the moisture will evaporate and then it will shrink, right?"

"Precisely! Now Mr. Scientist and Jr. Carpenter, let me show you how smart you really are! What if I had spread the putty out nice and smooth?"

"Uh, it would have shrunk, and then it would have been too low."

"Exactly! Well, you passed lesson number one in Science and Carpentry 101. Now let's put some books around this."

"What's the matter, we need smart putty instead of silly putty?" asked James.

"Oh, now we have a comedian, do we?" Gabe said as he reached over and ruffled James' hair. "No, the patch will have to sit for twenty-four hours before we can sand it. The books are to keep anyone from stepping in it. It is very important that no one disturb this patch understand?" James nodded that he did.

Jim and Fran arrived home a short time later and found Gabe diligently working around the door and James watching every move that he made.

"The door will be here first thing in the morning, Gabe," said Jim.

"That will be fine. I have a little work I have to do anyway before it arrives. You see, Mr. Whitman, we, I, had a little accident this afternoon."

"You what! What happened, was anybody

hurt?"

"Oh no, not at all."

Just about that time Jim spied the books and the damaged floor.

"What in the world happened here?" he yelled. "You were supposed to fix the place not tear it up!" Jim immediately turned and looked directly at James. "What did you do?" Jim said taking a step toward James. Jim had finally had enough of this nonsense and he knew without a doubt who had caused it. James began shaking his head negatively as his eyes filled with tears. James really was a 'basket case.' A straw basket of emotions and the emotions were about to burst through the woven straws of the basket.

Gabe cleared his throat loudly and said, "I'm so terribly sorry, Mr. Whitman, that it happened." Upon hearing Gabe, Jim seemed to deflate and return to a somewhat normal state. "I should have set my tool box on the floor. If you don't want me to return, I'll understand. But I would like to return long enough to finish repairing the floor. At no charge, of course, for the repair of the floor. I'll tell you what, Mr. Whitman. I'll finish the door and repair the floor. If you don't like my repair work, you don't have to pay me for any of my work. All you will owe me for is the materials. Deal?"

"Yeah, ok," Jim said smiling once again.

Gabe glanced in James direction and noticed the strained muscles in his face slowly begin to relax. He thought he actually saw James exhale a big breath of relief when his dad wasn't looking.

"Just make sure no one steps in this putty or rolls into it." Gabe said looking once again in James direction and winking at him.

"No problem," said James.

"Well I guess you could say I've done all the damage I can do here for one day. I'll come back at 7:30 in the morning to start work. If that's ok with you, of course?"

"Yeah, that will be fine," Jim remarked as he looked toward Fran for approval.

"Well, I'll gather my tools then and scat."

"Ok, that's fine. I'll see you in the morning. I have some things that I've got to do," Jim said as he turned and scurried off down the hallway.

"Sure," said Gabe.

Jim vanished down the hallway leaving Gabe and James alone once again.

"I'm sorry."

"What's that?" said Gabe.

"I said, I'm sorry. It was my fault that the tool-box fell. It wasn't your fault. Why did you take the blame? I mean, you didn't ever tell Dad that I had anything to do with it. You could even lose this job over the damage and you didn't do anything wrong, nothing at all. You were willing to take my punishment, and you didn't deserve it."

There was a long pause, and then Gabe turned his tender blue eyes toward James.

"You see, James, I did it because you are my friend. Maybe it's me that should apologize for getting so mad. My temper seems to be my downfall and my worse fault these days. I hardly ever get that angry but when I do; well you know. The damage had already been done and trying to cast blame wouldn't solve anything. There's always plenty of blame to go around anyway, in almost any situation. There's an old saying in the Bible, John 15:13 says 'No greater love hath a man than he lay down his life for a friend.'"

James sat quietly pondering what Gabe said for a minute as Gabe finished packing, but he really didn't know what to say. Finally, James just said, "Thanks." No one had ever stood with him like that before; especially when he was in the wrong.

Gabe headed for the door then stopped and turned toward James and said, "See you in the morning partner." Then winking his eye, Gabe continued, "Keep an eye on our project."

"Yeah, sure," said James. "I mean, yes sir," as James corrected himself.

Gabe turned and opened the door.

"Oh, Mr. Gabe," James shouted.

Gabe froze in his tracks and turned back to face James without saying a word.

"A while ago when I got the pry bar you said, "Congratulations." Why did you say that?"

Gabe sat his tools down, walked back over to James and knelt down where they could be eye to eye.

"First of all, James, you can just call me Gabe if you want to. Son, there are many kinds of prisons in this world. Some have bars, some are because of hate, and some even have wheels. The reason I said congratulations is because you are no longer a prisoner. You are only as handicapped as you make yourself feel. You are not an invalid. You are James Whitman, and you are not cripple anymore!"

Gabe muffed James' hair again as he stood up and walked toward the door.

"See 'ya' in the morning, tiger."

James didn't say a word, he just watched the door as it slowly closed and the latch clicked inside its housing.

James listened as the old truck cranked and backed out of the drive. In his mind he pictured the old truck driving down his street until he could no longer hear the roar of the engine. "Who was this old man?" It was as if James had known him all his life.

Gabe headed straight for the local pharmacy. Rubbing his head and wincing with pain, Gabe drove on, trying to keep the old truck on the road. He had been careful not to reveal how bad he felt. But he needed rest; he needed the strength it would provide him. As soon as he had his pain prescription refilled, he headed for home.

He pulled up at the empty old house and went inside. Scanning the desolate refrigerator, he selected his entrée for the evening. That evening he dined on an old, mellow apple, peanut butter and bread, and a glass of milk. Then as the sun was setting, he went to bed and listened to the tick of the old clock until it slowly faded away.

CHAPTER XVII

Jim and Fran couldn't figure out what was wrong with James. He was quiet all evening. Not one single item of food was thrown. He didn't eat much, and he even said, "Thank you," when his mother handed him his plate. His parents were almost upset by the change. They thought something must be terribly wrong with him. On the outside James was fine, but on the inside a vicious battle was raging. Once his mom even patted him on the hand but it was not a love pat. It was her way of checking to see if he possibly felt warm with a temperature.

All that evening James stayed within easy viewing of the patched floor. Anytime Jim or Fran came even remotely close, he would warn them to watch out. He had been assigned an important duty, and he had determined in his heart that he was not going to fail.

The next morning Jim was sleeping peacefully when Fran suddenly shocked him back into reality.

"Jim, Jim," Fran called softly but frantically, shaking him out of his peaceful slumber.

"Wake up, wake up, there's someone in the

house."

Fran had heard a noise five minutes earlier but had elected to wait before saying anything until she was sure of what it was. Not long afterward she had heard more noises. Gin wasn't home, and James never got up before ten. Since the accident, James had started staying up late and then sleeping all during the day. Jim and Fran hadn't said anything about it because he had become so hard to live with. Sadly, when James was asleep, it was the only time close to a normal life for the Whitman family. But now, it was almost daybreak and James would have gone to bed long ago.

Jim peered carefully down the hallway. Seeing no one, he slipped out the door and hugged the wall as he crept toward the noise in the living room. There in the shadows he could see something or someone moving around. Finally, his eyes began to focus on the dim figure as he peered into the blackness.

"It's okay, Dad, it's just me."

"James, oh boy, you gave me a start. I didn't even know you were out of bed. It's okay, Fran," he yelled back toward the bedroom. "It's James."

"Why are you up so early?" asked Jim.

"I just couldn't sleep, and I just wanted to check and make sure the patch was ok."

Before Jim could say another word, James locked both wheels into place and spun his whole body around in his chair by pushing up on the chair's arms. Slowly he twisted and squirmed until he was out of the chair and down on the floor. Breathless he reached over and caressed the rough patch as if it were a little kitten.

"He was right," James said. "It did shrink."

The mound of putty was now at a level just above the floor. It was also hard just like the wood on the floor. Jim was stunned. He hadn't seen James put forth effort like that since their baseball championship.

After he was satisfied that the patch was firm and locked into place, James turned and began pulling himself back toward his chair. Jim started toward him and was going to help lift him into the chair.

"No," said James. "I can do it myself."

Jim stepped back. "I know you can, James, but if you'll just let me help a little."

Again, James shouted, "No, I don't need your help. Just leave me alone, I'm not handicapped!"

Jim turned like a whipped puppy and reluctantly headed back to his bedroom. As he lay in bed nursing his wounds, he listened carefully for a crash in case he was needed.

Just as Dr. Fredericks had said, they had ridden an emotional roller coaster for months. They were all frustrated not knowing how or when or even if the ride would ever end. Jim kept thinking, "All I wanted to do was to help him. I love him so much. Why didn't I make him wear his seat belt? I'm the grown up; I knew better. Why wasn't it me instead of James in that chair?" Jim continued to listen for the crash, ready to leap up and save the day, but it never happened. Finally, Jim drifted back off to sleep.

James was bored stiff. He found the remote control and started scanning the channels. The television gave off an eerie blue glow in the darkened room.

I wonder what time the sun comes up?" he whispered to himself. The first channel had a muscle-bound beauty queen working out on a stair climber.

"Come on, you can do it," she pleaded, "pump those legs!" Then miraculously she was transported to a beautifully landscaped garden in Hawaii. In one hand she held a book, and in the other her latest workout video. James didn't hear what she said at first, but her last words resounded in his ears.

"If you follow the simple guidelines outlined in my book or my new tape, you can walk your way into health. What's holding you back? Get out of that chair and start moving. Remember, that's only $29.95 for the cassette or both for only---."

Her words trailed off as the blood began to pound in his ears. He drew his arm back, ready to missile the remote at the television, but instead he forced himself to calm down and slowly allowed his arm to rest on the padded arm of the chair.

He pressed the channel up button again on the remote.

"Yes, that's right. If you'll just attend one of my free seminars, you, too, can become a millionaire."

The next channel was another exercise program. This one happened to be on the beach. He quickly bypassed the one after that, too, with their psychic friends.

The following channel brought the sound of a table saw ripping a board into the room.

"You must be extra careful," said the man, "when ripping a long board. It's best to have someone else guide the stock straight off the table. So find a friend and get to building."

James was fascinated. For thirty minutes he watched the man cut board after board on the saw. He had never seen a saw like it before.

Next a woman walked in and said she had a table with a broken leg that needed to be repaired.

James was spellbound as he watched her prepare the stock and mount it on a lathe. At first the wood turned around and around very slowly, yet it still looked blurry as he watched it spin. The lady then slowly eased a tool up next to it while resting it on a flat edged bar she called a fence. She said the tool was called a gouge and she explained how important it was to hold the gouge with two hands and to slowly let it shave off the sharp edges of the board. Next, she sped the lathe up a little and turned the stock down to a cylinder.

James knew what a cylinder was. He had studied about it in math. Faster and faster the wood spun around as she worked it down. She really had the chips flying.

James thought he would really like to try using a lathe. Next, she worked it down to where the stock was basically the shape of the table leg. James hardly blinked, he was completely mesmerized. He figured that this must also be the way wooden baseball bats were made. He would have to remember to ask Gabe to see if he was correct. He watched until the show was over.

"Make sure and tune in tomorrow when we'll be refinishing old wooden floors."

Then James really became excited.

James kept flipping channels but couldn't find anything else interesting after the handy-man show went off. Finally, he just turned the television off. He looked at the clock. It was 6:50, Gabe should be here soon. He couldn't wait to tell him about the show he saw.

Every time James heard an engine, he sat up and listened intently only to hear it fade away into the distance. Car after car went by, and even a truck drove past, but it wasn't Gabe. Eventually, James' ear caught a brief sound that was familiar. Way off in the distance he could hear a low rumble. He listened as carefully as possible. "Yes," he thought, "it sounds like his truck. It has to be it." He heard the old body rattle as the truck crossed over the railroad tracks one block over. The sound was coming right in his direction.

Then suddenly a gust of wind or a house or something blocked the sound, and for a second it faded away. James almost panicked. But just as suddenly as it disappeared, it once more resounded closer than ever. The brakes squealed as the old truck slowed at the corner and then squealed again as it turned into the drive.

The engine coughed once and then died. The old door once again creaked open and slowly closed as it had thousands of times before. James quietly pulled down the open window he had raised in order to listen for the truck and rolled his chair over in the direction of the door.

Footsteps approached the door and could be heard systematically scraping on the door mat outside. Then a soft but firm tapping echoed through the door.

James yelled, "Come in."

Gabe cracked the door open just enough to stick his head inside.

"Is the coast clear," Gabe said softly trying not to awaken anyone who may still be sleeping.

Gabe stepped inside and quietly closed the door.

"Tell your mom and dad that I am here, okay?"

James cupped his hands to his mouth and began to draw in a deep breath.

"No, no," said Gabe. "Don't scream it, go tell them."

"That's stupid," thought James. "It's so much easier to yell."

Knowing what James was about to do, Gabe said, "Yes, I know. But it's more polite this way."

James rolled down the hall as Gabe started laying out his tools. Then he walked over to the shelf on the wall.

"They're up," said James as he rolled back into the room.

James looked at Gabe's hands. Cradled in

his hands was the golden trophy that James had broken all to pieces. It looked brand new.

"How did you do it?" James asked.

"A lot of patience and understanding along with a lot of super glue and gold paint."

"But that still doesn't answer my question. It looks new. I mean it's perfect. I really annihilated that guy. I thought he was history. He was trash."

"Son, it's hard to say. Some people call me a master carpenter, and I don't know that I necessarily agree with them. One day, though, if you work really hard, you can be a master at whatever you do. Whatever you choose, whether it's electronics, medicine, preaching, or even fishing, if you'll do your best and learn your field from top to bottom and through and through, people will see your work and know that the master has touched it."

Gabe carefully set the man and his marble base back up on his pedestal.

"How's that patch looking James?"

"It did just what you said it would do. It's almost level with the floor."

Gabe dropped to one knee and felt the patch.

"Yep, that's just about right. 'Gotta' work her down a bit though. Be right back."

Gabe went back to the truck and came back

with an old, electric sander. The old cord was cracked and all taped up.

"How old is that thing?" James asked.

"Well, it didn't come over on the ark, but it might have made the second load," laughed Gabe. This is a reciprocating sander. It moves back and forth, not around like an orbital sander. An orbital sander would cut across the grain and may leave scratches in the floor. This one will sand with the grain and help the patch to blend in better.

Gabe showed James how to measure and cut the sandpaper and load it onto the sander. Then he turned the sander on and let James see its action. It moved back and forth so fast it just became a blur. James tried to fix his eyes on one spot and after a few seconds said, "Wow, that kind of makes me dizzy just watching it."

With the sander running, it sounded like a giant bumble bee. Gabe reached down once more and ran his hand over the hump. Turning off the sander, Gabe said come over here and feel the patch and how it is raised. James wheeled over and once again contorted himself and slid out of his chair and onto the floor. Sliding his hand across the smooth floor, his hand stopped as it hit the patch and James had to raise his hand slightly to slide it over the hump. Afterward, Gabe too reached down to gauge the height of the hump and how much he would need to take off.

Carefully and resolutely Gabe eased the instrument down toward the patient. The hump and sander met and clashed in a terrible conflict. Dust rose and sifted across the floor as if from some great battle. Slowly the small mountain relented to its conqueror. When it was almost level, Gabe said, "James, take the scissors out of my tool box and cut me another piece of sandpaper but this time use the medium grade." After measuring, cutting, and installing the sandpaper, Gabe bragged about what a good job he had done. "See how important school is now," said Gabe. "You have to use all the school subjects at some time in your life. You just used Math, Reading, and Science to help cut that paper." James got very quiet as he pondered Gabe's words.

"Now, it's your turn," Gabe said as he handed the sander to James. James acted surprised as he took the sander from Gabe. James turned on the switch and laughed at the way it made his hands feel as the sander vibrated. Carefully, he let the sander down onto the remaining hump on the floor. He was very careful to only sand with the grain of the wood.

After a few minutes Gabe said, "that's good, let's check it occasionally before we sand it too deep."

Repeatedly, James sanded and stopped then

sanded and stopped again.

When it was just right Gabe announced that it was close enough.

Now we've got to get acquainted with the wood," said Gabe.

"We've got to what?" questioned James.

"The wood is almost level now. We have to be very careful from this point on."

Gabe took a piece of fine sandpaper and a wooden block and after wrapping the paper around the block, began systematically to work down the wood. James watched carefully. Gabe must have started and stopped sanding twenty-five times. After sanding for a few seconds, Gabe would take his hand and caress the surface of the wood. Five times Gabe let James feel the wood as he carefully honed it away. To watch Gabe work you would have thought he was cutting diamonds.

Gabe finally looked up and smiled, then stepped back and said, "That's it."

"You mean we're finished?" asked James. "It doesn't look very good."

"Oh, no," said Gabe. "We're finished with part one. But I'll let you do step two all by yourself if you think you can handle it."

"If you'll show me, I bet I can."

"Good, I'll be right back."

Gabe returned carrying a small, red vacuum cleaner.

"All right, here it is champ."

"What? You want me to clean up!"

"It won't kill you."

James took the vacuum cleaner even though there was a look of great displeasure on his face.

"It may seem like something small or unimportant but cleaning up and organizing your work may be one of the most important things you do on any job," said Gabe.

"Now be especially careful around the patch," continued Gabe.

James took the vacuum and cleaned the area thoroughly all around the patch and then very carefully on the patch itself. He looked every few seconds for an affirmation from Gabe that it was enough and the job was done. After a couple of minutes Gabe looked his way and smiled and James knew that his task was completed.

"Thanks, good job" said Gabe. "You don't realize how important this is. We'll probably do this two or three more times before we varnish the floor. If you do any sealing or varnishing with a lot of dust around, the dust will find its way into the varnish and cloud the finish. Then the patch would stick out like a sore thumb. You know James, it's kind of the same way with people when you think about it."

"What do you mean?" asked James.

"Well, think of the people who you consider to be the most successful. Note, I didn't say the ones who were the most famous or have the most money. That's not really success. Think about the people who are the happiest and the most content. Those are the successful people. Those are the people with a good finish like the clear varnish that we want. Now think about the people who are not so happy. James, you tell me something that causes them hurt or causes them to be unhappy."

"I don't know, um drugs maybe, alcohol, divorce, um---"

"Yeah, that's right! Can you think of any more?"

"How about greed; you know wanting more all the time. Hey, that's kind of like the dust and dirt in the varnish, it messes up the clear finish."

"Boy, you are a fast learner. Bad things do happen to good people. We can't always control what happens to us. Things that happen to us are not always our fault.

You're right though, it's the trash that gets into our lives that clouds our finish. We have to keep the junk out of our lives so that we, too, can have a shining finish. Something that's just as important, though, is having a good attitude."

"How's that so important?"

"You know that brand new truck that I drive?"

James almost burst out laughing thinking about the old, dented and faded, worn down truck.

"Okay, okay," said Gabe. "It wasn't that funny. That old truck gets me where I'm going and keeps me warm. True, it doesn't have beautiful colors or a flashy logo on the side. But it's paid for. Yes, it would be nice to have a new truck. But I don't have to have one to be happy. Some folks have to have a new truck every year or two or die. Then every month they have to wring their hands wondering how they will ever make the payments. Their family and even they themselves often have to live half a life, having needs unmet because they wanted something they didn't need. They get upset and make everyone around them miserable."

"So, you see, happiness is an attitude. It's up to you to make yourself happy. Don't depend on others or what they can do for you to make you happy. You've probably heard it said, 'I complained because I had no shoes until I met a man who had no feet.' James, you can use that chair as an anchor or as a springboard. You can let it hold you back, or you can use it to take you to the moon. You may sit a little lower than most folks, but remember happiness is not an altitude; it's an attitude, and you have it inside, if you'll just use it."

Everything was quiet once more in the house. The only sound was the steady tick, tick, tick of the old clock on the mantle.

After a moment Gabe broke the silence. James had enough to chew on for a while.

"Better not feed him too much just yet," thought Gabe.

"Now it's time for step three on our patch. What do you notice about our patch that's different from the rest of the floor?"

"Well, it's not shiny. Besides that, it's kind of funny shaped and doesn't match the boards in the floor."

"Let's see what we can do about that."

Gabe went back to his truck and brought back a tool that looked like a big "L" with little marks all over it kind of like a ruler.

"What's that for?" asked James.

"This is called a framing square, and it's used to keep things straight and to build rafters and stairs."

"If someone bopped me on the head with that thing, it would make me straighten up!" laughed James nervously trying to be funny.

Gabe took the square and laid it over the patch

lining it up with the other boards on the floor. Then he took out a box cutter with a razor blade and cut thin, shallow, straight lines into the patch lining it up with the other boards in the floor. Completing his last cut, Gabe took a piece of fine sandpaper and gently went over the lines and the patch once more. It actually was looking more and more just like the real floor.

"There's something else missing James, what is it?"

"I don't know. The putty just doesn't look like the real boards."

"Be right back," said Gabe. He took the framing square back and tucked it away safely. Returning to the living room, Gabe produced a stiff wire brush and a can of dark stain.

"You see this flooring has little holes called pores in it. You'll learn all about that in science."

Gabe took the steel brush and with three quick, rough strokes said, "Wala. Instant pores my friend." With three light strokes of the sandpaper, he declared the sanding at an end. Lastly, he had James once more vacuum the patch. Out of his pocket Gabe took a little, short brush about the size of a pencil. Gabe pried open a can of dark stain and just barely dipped the tip of the brush into it. Carefully and meticulously he painted the stain onto the putty in a "flame" pattern to match the rest of the board and the pattern that would have been there had it not been gouged out by the tool box.

"Wow!" said James. "You can hardly tell the difference."

"That's all for about thirty minutes. The door hasn't

arrived yet, so I tell you what, let's go outside for a while."

"Why?"

"Just to get you out of the house; don't you like being outside?" asked Gabe.

"Go to your room and get your glove and a ball," said Gabe.

"Are you kidding me. I can't play baseball."

"Oh yeah, I forgot you're handicapped!"

CHAPTER XVIII

James was furious and almost cursed his new friend. With his teeth clinched, he spun his chair around and headed down the hall. A few minutes later he returned with a glove and a ball. He had made a lot of noise searching for them. It had been a long time since he'd had them out and they had migrated to the bottom and to the back of his closet.

Gabe was careful and helped him ease out of the chair and onto the couch. Then Gabe carefully folded the chair, eased it through the narrow door, and re-opened it outside. Grabbing James under the arms, he weakly drug him out to the chair. With a mighty lunge, Gabe lifted him to his seat. Breathless, Gabe leaned on the chair for support.

James was shocked at the sight of him as he struggled and coughed, trying to catch his breath.

"Are you ok?" James asked; his temper now assuaged and looking more concerned than angry.

"Yes," Gabe panted, "I'll be fine in just a minute.

Gabe soon caught his breath and down the ramp they went. After pushing James to the middle of the front yard, Gabe said, "Hold on, and I'll be right back."

James heard him still breathing heavily as he lumbered off toward the truck.

Gabe went back to the old truck and reached under the seat. From beneath the seat he took out something wrapped in cloth. When he unwrapped it, it appeared to be the remnants of an old glove. He opened the glove and slipped it onto his left hand.

"What's that?" asked James. "Oh, don't tell me. You had that glove when you were in school, and you caught a homerun ball in the World Series in '36'."

"No, smarty pants. I didn't have this glove when I was in school, and I caught the homerun in '37' not '36,' so see there, you don't know every-thing!"

James was sitting with his mouth open.

"Did you really catch a ball in the '37' Series?"

"Are you kidding? I may have caught a cold in '37' but that's about all!"

After locking eyes for a few seconds, they both burst out laughing. Gabe stepped off about thirty steps and said, "Are you ready?"

"Yeah, I'm ready for 'ya' old timer. Come on, ring my bell. Put my lights ou---."

James didn't have time to finish his sentence because he had to protect himself from the fastball that was meteoring toward his chest. In a flash he had the glove up and caught the ball.

"Hey, you trying to kill somebody or something?"

"What did you want, a little sissy toss or something? You used to be a state champ! But, if it pleases his highness, I'll throw the next one underhanded."

"Hey, watch the smart talk, old man!"

"Who you calling 'old man,' boy?"

"Who are you calling 'boy'?" relied James.

They both started grunting and bowing up like they were going to fight. Then looking each other in the eye again, they both burst into laughter a second time.

They spent the next thirty minutes throwing the ball. Gabe had intentionally put James behind a small mound in the yard. He not only threw pitches but also high balls and grounders. When the ball hit the hump on the ground, it would suddenly take flight right toward James' face.

James was handling them all like a pro. He had just caught a sizzler and was about to return it in like fashion when Gabe suddenly grabbed his head with his hands and began to squeeze tightly. Gabe's face began to distort and wrinkle with pain as he dropped to his knees.

Quickly James released the locks on his wheels and raced towards him as fast as the soft grass would allow.

"Gabe, Gabe are you all right?"

For a few seconds Gabe didn't respond. Then slowly the wrinkles on his forehead began to relax, and his face began to return to normal. Slowly he rose to his feet. In the back of his mind Gabe knew that he was on his last mission. There was one more boy, another family to rescue. "Please Lord," Gabe thought to himself. "Please let me finish. Let me do this one last job."

"Just a sudden pain that caught me off guard. It's nothing to worry about. I'll be fine in a minute. Just give me another second."

"Are you sure we don't need to call an ambulance or something? You don't look so good."

"So, now you are going to start making fun of my looks," Gabe said as he began to straighten up.

While he waited for Gabe to regain his strength, James started looking all around him. It was beautiful outside. It was still winter, but the sun was bright, and there was just enough coolness in the air to make it crisp. Over across the yard was an old maple which still fought desperately to retain a few of its brilliant leaves. James thought it strange since the other maples had dropped their leaves weeks ago. He looked at all the other maples around their property. They looked like skeletons standing guard over him. They gave him goose-bumps and forced him to direct his attention back to the beautiful maple in the front yard.

His eyes followed the trunk down to Gabe's old truck which was parked beneath it. On the side of the truck was a hand-painted sign that said, "Gabe's rolling fix-it shop. If you can break it, I can fix it." Deep inside, James was beginning to realize just how prophetic the words were.

James' concentration was suddenly broken when someone started calling his name.

"Hey Dad, what's the matter?" replied James.

"I need to speak with you, and Gabe needs to get back to work. Gabe, the hardware store called and said the door would be here in fifteen minutes."

James looked at his dad as if paying attention, but he was listening closer to the crunch of the gravel and the old truck door groaning once more as it was roused from its slumber. He imagined Gabe meticulously rewrapping the glove in cloth and tucking it neatly back under the truck seat.

"James, I met with your principal and your teachers before the holidays. We all agreed that it's time for you to get back to school. The school board has agreed to make an attendance exception if you return to school immediately and maintain a B average for the rest of the year. If you don't maintain a B average, you will be required to repeat the 7th grade."

James had a very solemn look on his face. He knew this day would come, but he hoped it would be a long time off.

"Well, when would I have to go back?"

"Monday, son, right after the Christmas holidays."

"But the kids will make fun of me and call me names!"

"We've already tried to take care of that. A counselor is going to talk to your class Monday morning, and if you like, she'll talk to you as well."

"Why can't I just stay here?"

"Now James, you know that's impossible. Besides, there is a state compulsory attendance law that says that you have to go to school until you're sixteen."

"I guess I can take it two and a half more years. But when I turn sixteen, I'm 'outta' there."

Jim feeling the blood begin to rise in his face said, "Now James, I'm not going to tell you this but once. I want—"

"Mr. Whitman, I believe I see the delivery truck coming with your door," Gabe butted in. "I may need you to help me for a few minutes."

"Yeah, uh sure, whatever."

Jim Whitman had lost his composure. He tried to regain his previous countenance but for some reason he just couldn't bring back the voracious lion like attitude that had just fled him."

"James, uh, we'll talk about this later."

Then Jim strode off toward the delivery truck. The truck began making an obnoxious beeping noise as it slowly backed down the drive.

James looked up at Gabe, "Thanks," he said.

Gabe winked back, "Don't mention it."

As soon as Jim helped Gabe take down the old door, he disappeared to complete a few errands. Gabe had already taken notice of the polished set of golf clubs in Jim's backseat. "Nice day for a round," thought Gabe.

Soon afterward, Fran appeared and said that she had to have a few things from the store.

"Gin should be here soon, Mr. Michaels. Would you mind if I leave for a little while since you're going to be here anyway?"

"No, no, that's fine. By the way, Fran, have you ever played any golf?"

"No, not really, why?"

"I believe you will find Jim at the course. Why don't you surprise him and drive his cart for him? I'm sure he'd like the company, and I can take care of things around here. Go ahead, you deserve a break."

"Well, it is a pretty day. That's what I used to do when we were dating. I may just take you up on that and see if I can still manage to drive a cart."

Fran went back inside for a light jacket, said goodbye, and left in the car.

"That'll do them good," said James as he sat staring off into space. "They need to get away from me. Besides, I don't need a babysitter anyway. I don't need anyone."

"You're exactly right," said Gabe.

"What?" said James, who had been seeking sympathy, not someone to agree with him.

"Well, it's true," said Gabe.

"It's not that they don't love you, and it's not the chair. If Gin were standing here, I could have still said the same thing. It's good for everyone to get away sometime, if for nothing else, just to think and be alone. They still need times like that even though they have been married for a long time. Don't take it personal. Besides, we need to finish our patch. But first, we have to finish framing in the new door."

Gabe spent the next hour and a half framing in the door. Most of the preparations had already been made. When he finished, he had James vacuum the patch again.

Then they took more stain that was identical to the stain on the floor and re-stained the whole patch.

"Boy, that looks good," said James.

"Yes, I have to agree, it's looking better all the time. Tomorrow we'll varnish it."

There was a noise just outside the door as Gin shuffled up the sidewalk.

"Well, look who decided to show up, somebody kill the fattened calf, the prodigal sister has returned."

Gin entered the door with her hand on her hip and a smirk on her face. Before she could say a word, James said, "Well. Here's the fattened calf; where's the sister?"

"James, don't you even start with me."

"What's the matter, you can dish it out, but you can't take it!"

"James," Gabe said firmly.

James instantly hushed and asked, "Sir?"

"I'm surprised at you son!"

Gin was standing, but felt weak in the knees. She had never seen James act this way. He didn't argue; he didn't talk back; why, he wasn't even sarcastic.

"Are you all right, Gin?" asked Gabe.

She hadn't realized how dumbfounded she looked standing there with her mouth gaping open.

"Yeah, uh, Yes sir, I'm fine."

James just sat there looking like a whipped puppy.

"James, a great leader never chides, ridicules, or mocks his troops or his followers."

"Do what?" asked Gin. "What did you say? His followers, you've got to be kidding me. I wouldn't follow him to---"

Gabe just reached out, took Gin's arm in his, and patted her arm firmly but gently to let her know to be quiet.

" 'Capn' Gabe Michaels and Private Gin Whitman reporting for duty, Sir." Gabe barked out as he made a quick and snappy salute.

"Now wait just a 'cotton-pickin' minute! I don't answer to any kid who tells me what to do and especially not to him!" Gin said, crossing her arms.

"Sir, there appears to be some dissention in the ranks. May I have a minute with the private sir?" asked Gabe.

"Private, my foot, I don't know what kind of a game you're playing but I won't have---"

Gabe turned and whispered to Gin, "Now Gin, you're going to have to trust me on this one, even if you don't want too. Everything will be fine, I promise."

They turned expecting to face a whipped puppy, but instead they met General Patton reborn. James looked as if he were ready to spit fire and bark orders. If he'd had fatigues and two pearl-handled pistols, he could have acted out Patton's role to the hilt.

"We are ready for your orders, sir," Gabe said standing at attention. It was an easy role for Gabe to play. He had done it many times before. At home, tucked safely away in a drawer were his purple heart and Congressional Medal of Honor that he had been awarded in World War II. He had many adventurous stories to share with friends over the years. One of his favorites happened not long after he made it to Europe. It was somewhat of a miracle that he was even here to retell the story.

CHAPTER XIX

Gabe's platoon had been ambushed early one cold October morning in 1944. With their radio destroyed and all hope lost, a young Gabe volunteered to try to go for help. Most of the other men were either wounded or exhausted. All day long they had held their position, precarious as it was. Had the Germans known how weak the platoon really was, they would have over-run them easily. As night began to fall and the first cool wisp of evening air began to filter down into the little gorge where they were held up, their sergeant could hear the German soldiers laughing and ridiculing the Americans all around their perimeter.

It sounded as if there were a German soldier behind every tree and rock surrounding the camp. With only a forty-five-caliber pistol borrowed from the sarge along with two clips of ammo and a canteen of water, Gabe crept out of the safety of the cluster of rocks and trees that he had been hiding behind. He crawled and scurried from shadow to shadow until he thought he was getting near the Germans. Even then, Gabe showed wisdom far beyond his years.

All day he had watched and listened to every move the enemy had made. His adversaries knew that the platoon was pinned down and all they had to do was just wait them out until they surrendered. The Germans were overconfident and continuously gave away their positions with their laughter and ridiculing. Gabe kept noticing smoke back toward the north all day long. The Germans had settled in for the long haul and taking the opportunity to break from their battlefield rations, had actually set up a temporary kitchen. At different times Gabe could actually smell food cooking. He knew too that the prospect of a hot meal would draw the soldiers to the kitchen like flies. Once or twice the Germans had actually taunted the Americans by calling out in very broken English for the Americans to come and join them for lunch.

Being an old country boy from Georgia, Gabe figured it only made sense that if the kitchen was at one end of the camp, then the temporary latrine must be somewhere at the other end. He was willing to bet that late in the evening more of the soldiers would be gathered around the cook pot than the other pot. So he made a bee line for where he figured the latrine area would be located. He also figured that this would be where the fewest number of soldiers would want to be stationed. It also made sense that the brightest and highest-ranking officers would be nowhere around the area. The only soldiers stationed here would be the only ones not smart enough to talk their way out of it.

When Gabe had gone as far as he felt relatively safe to go, his nose told him exactly what he wanted to know. He was right on target. Looking at his watch he whispered, "Two minutes to go." Carefully he stretched his legs so they wouldn't go to sleep as he waited for the diversion to begin. The last few seconds he counted down mentally, "5,4,3,2,1."

With the first shot, Gabe was off like a flash. He ran between the trees to provide some cover for himself. Rounding a large rock, he was suddenly knocked to the ground. He had unfortunately or fortunately, stumbled right through the latrine.

The young German private laying on the ground just five feet away had eyes as big as saucers. He had quickly stood up as soon as he heard the first shot only to be knocked flat by the quarterback from the other team. Now he lay on the ground panting in utter disbelief at what had happened. He had never seen an American soldier this close before, and he was scared to death.

Quickly with one hand, he clumsily started clawing at the dirt and kicking the ground trying to get away. With his other hand he was frantically trying to get his pants pulled back up. There have been many occasions since that time when Gabe and his friends have laughed themselves to tears over the incident.

That day, however, was not as jovial. Gabe had been running with his pistol clasped in his hand. When the collision had occurred, he was only down for a second and then he was back up aiming his pistol at the green recruit on the ground. The young German, only slightly more than a boy himself, glanced and calculated the distance between himself and his rifle leaning against a nearby rock. Gabe quickly picked up on his intentions as he noticed the nervousness in the German's rapidly darting blue eyes. Gabe shook his head "no," at the private and lifted the pistol higher where the young German could get a better look at it. The German seemed to wilt at the futility and embarrassment of his situation and he relaxed his taunt muscles. Gabe pointed the gun at the German's pants and motioned for him to pull them up. Gabe could see the appreciation in his eyes as he regained some of his pride.

Gabe stepped to the side and picked up the rifle. Wedging it between two rocks, he gave it a firm push placing a slight curve in the barrel. Any German soldier using that rifle in the future never would be able to figure out why he could never hit what or whoever he aimed at.

"Well, that's one rifle that will never kill another GI," thought Gabe.

Gabe raised a single finger to his lips as if to tell the German to, "be quiet." Then Gabe raised his hand in a salute and took off. The German soldier remained on the ground shocked and astonished at what had just happened and thanking God and in a way Gabe, for sparing his life.

Like a gazelle, Gabe was off, running for his life. Once he glanced back over his shoulder, but the soldier was still frozen to the ground and Gabe realized that this was his one and probably only chance to get away.

Gabe knew that not only his life was in jeopardy but also all the men waiting back in the gorge were in jeopardy. He also knew that they were counting on him and that he was their last hope. He couldn't let them down. Failure meant their death or worse, their capture. He began to run faster, faster than he had ever run in his life.

He wasn't too worried about the German soldier. After all, what would he say? To the Germans, Gabe was just an American coward gone AWOL trying to save his own skin. They say in Germany today there is still an old war veteran who regales his grandchildren with their favorite story about when he was in the war and caught an American spy trying to infiltrate their lines. The children laugh with glee when he tells them how fast the American ran away when their grandfather discovered him; how the American was no match for the mighty German army.

All night Gabe ran using only a compass and the stars as a guide. The only times he rested were to get a bearing on his location and to take a quick sip of water. Then he was off again. Several times he had almost lunged right into enemy camps, but somehow, he managed to get through.

Early the next morning the Germans awoke to the rumble of tanks coming down the road right toward their encampment. Assuming they were their own tanks, many of the German soldiers casually walked out to the road to watch the mighty German Panzer Division pass by. To their dismay, what rounded the corner was indeed something to behold. Not just one or two but twelve, new modern Sherman tanks with a great, big, white star from the good old USA. Most of the Germans had not even stopped to pick up their rifles. Everyone of them turned like scared jack rabbits and high tailed it into the woods without even firing a single shot.

In the lead tank, leading the way, was a young GI, battle-scarred from his brush with death. He risked it all, even his own life for those he loved.

Gabe thought it was so ironic that now Germany was one of the United States' greatest allies. He attributed this to the kindness of the Marshall Plan and the compassion of some of the troops such as "The Candy Bomber" for the German children.

For many years, men from the platoon called or wrote their hero on a regular basis. Some of them sent him pictures of children or grandchildren named Gabe or Gabriel. The letters had gotten fewer and fewer over the years. Now he only received one or two every couple of years. Gabe figured that most of the men were dead now, lost to the ages of so many that had died serving the country they loved. He liked the way General Douglas MacArthur had put it. When he retired from the service, he said, "Old soldiers never die; they just fade away." Still it was comforting to think that maybe something he'd done had helped to give them an appreciation of how precious life really is. These days, Gabe thought of death more often than not. After the war was over there were days that guilt haunted him. He asked himself many times why he got to come home when so many of his friends didn't. There were so many, even now that were buried in foreign fields or were never found. Gabe hoped when his time came that it wouldn't be alone in some sterile hospital or nursing facility. He wanted to die as he had lived, doing something worthwhile, doing something to help someone else, to make the world a better place.

General James' first order to Gabe was to stain the door and the molding around it.

"Yes, sir," said Gabe. Gabe had already finished preparing the surface for staining. Next, he showed Gin how to apply the stain, and he gave James a piece of cloth to stain with as well. Within the hour the staining was completed.

"Well, General, where are we off to now?"

"Uh, I don't know," said James.

Gabe looking off into the distance said, "We could sail the Seven Seas or sail on the Queen Mary, or maybe get shipwrecked on a deserted island. So, what will it be, Admiral?" asked Gabe.

In as deep and gruff voice as possible, James announced, "To sail the Seven Seas and see the wonders of the world, my good man."

"To the sea it is then, my captain."

Gin's head was in a blur.

"What do you mean, what's going on?" said Gin.

"You heard him, Gin," said James. "We're going to sail the world."

"Gin, write your parents a note and tell them that we're sailing the seven seas, but we will be back by supper."

Bewildered, Gin looked at Gabe as if he had totally lost his mind. She didn't say a word or make a move. She just froze in her steps.

"Remember, just trust me Gin."

"All right, all right, Mom and Dad said you did a few odd things, but they did say you were nice and that I could trust you."

"Oh, um, let me see that note when you finish with it, ok?" Gin reached over and handed the note to him. Quickly he scanned it and then wrote something else at the bottom.

"Ok, that's it, we're off. There's no use in sitting around and watching the stain dry! The day is much too nice to stay here. There's no stopping us now!"

Gabe pushed James out the newly widened door with Gin closely in tow. Gin locked the door while Gabe pushed James over to the truck.

Looking at the truck, Gin said, "You don't really think I'm going to ride in this old truck!"

"What truck?" said Gabe.

"You know very well what truck I'm talking about!"

"This is not a truck," said Gabe. "It's an M-1 tank filled with high tech weaponry and sophisticated guidance systems to get us to our destination."

"Oh, brother," said Gin.

Gin and Gabe helped James into the truck and then loaded his chair into the back. They drove about five miles. At first Gin was so embarrassed she wanted to crawl under the seat. After a while, though, she began to forget about what people might think and just relaxed and let her hair fly in the wind. "Anyway, what does it matter what people think when you are headed for the Seven Seas."

CHAPTER XX

Gabe drove down winding dirt roads deeper and deeper into the forest. The farther they drove, the more beautiful it became. They saw all kinds of wildlife, squirrels, hawks, and even a white-tailed deer with a little spotted fawn that pranced across the road in front of them. The deer paused only a second, swished her tail a couple of times as she stared at the slowly approaching vehicle, then she gamboled off through the clear pine forest as graceful as a ballerina. She stopped only a moment to look back to ensure that her fawn was following in her tracks. Gabe looked at the wide-eyed youngsters.

"We must be going to have an early Spring; you don't usually see a fawn this early." Gabe drew in a deep breath of the country air. "Welcome to heaven," he said. "At least the closest thing to it here on earth."

James and Gin had lived mostly in large towns and cities all their lives. For them, this experience was something to hold and savor for eternity. They breathed in deeply the pine-scented air. They noticed a sudden change in the air as they crossed a narrow, wooden bridge over a dark, bubbling, little creek. The air was sweet and heavy and, it drew you in and invited you to stay.

Finally, they came to a little road that turned to the right and drove up to a steel cable that hung limply across the road. Gabe got out of the truck and unfastened the cable allowing it to drop to the ground. They drove over it and headed deeper into the forest. The trees and wild shrubs began to close in on the old truck. Branches began to brush its sides as the road grew smaller and smaller. It was as if the forest were trying to swallow the old truck and make it a part of itself. The infrequently traveled road finally became so narrow they had to roll up the windows to keep the limbs from reaching inside the truck and grabbing them.

Further and further they pushed on, running over tall weeds and grasses as they marched onward. Just as it had thickened, the forest just as suddenly began to thin and open up. The forest had actually made it look almost like sunset because the canopy of the trees was so thick. Now it was as if an entirely new day was being born. The sky became blue, and the sun was shining once more in all of its glory.

Ahead they saw an old rusty tin roof reaching up from the forest floor. It was a part of an earlier era and was fighting for its very survival against all the elements. It appeared to be a losing battle as it was slowly being absorbed by the deep woods.

The thick road gave way to a little clearing covered with thick brown grass.

"It's not much," said Gabe, "but it's mine." As they approached the house and parked, the trees opened up on the left side, and there before them were all the postcards Gin had ever seen blended together into one beautiful scene. Spread before them was a lake as black as a moonless night. Guarding its shores were ancient cypress and tupelo trees. The gray Spanish moss which draped their old and majestic branches swayed gently in the breeze.

"Pretty aren't they?" Gabe said. "I call them, 'The Waiters,' because of the way they line the lake all dressed up with towels over their bent arms. When I come up with a 'mess of fish,' I always say, like the waiters, 'Dinner is served.'"

The lake was long and narrow and appeared to go on forever.

"Are we the only ones here?" asked James.

"Most likely," said Gabe. "There are a few other cabins around but most folks are caught up in their jobs and getting rich when all the riches are right here, right below their noses, waiting on them and they hardly ever come."

Gabe and Gin helped James out of the truck and into his chair. Gabe said, "Hold on, and I'll be right back." He disappeared into the old tin house and returned with poles and fishing equipment for all three of them. Setting the tackle box in James' lap, he said, "Here, you carry this." James gave him kind of a funny look. "Well," said Gabe, "You didn't think you were going to get off 'scot-free,' did you? Everybody has to pull his weight around here." James just smiled and shrugged his shoulders.

They walked down to the edge of the water and found an old boat chained to a tree. Gabe took a large ring of keys from his pocket and unlocked the rusty old padlock that was keeping the boat fastened to the tree. It was obvious that Gabe had been here recently. In the front of the boat Gabe had fastened a seat with two seat belts on it for James. Also, in the boat were three lifejackets and paddles.

Gabe explained to James that, should the boat turn over, the seatbelts could be released just like those in a car. "As a matter of fact, I got them out of a junk car at the wrecking yard."

"Gin," Gabe said, "I also have some special instructions for you. I want you to put this note in your pocket."

"What is it, what's it all about?"

Gabe sighed, "Not that I expect anything to happen to me, but you never know. If something should happen to me, then read the note."

"Nothing is going to happen to you. Why

should it?" said Gin.

"I could fall out of the boat or have a heart attack or any number of things. I'm no young chicken, you know. By the way, the keys to the truck are in the ashtray. Well, let's quit all the gabbing and get to fishing. We can't catch anything standing here."

They strapped James in and cast off. The boat cut through the water noiselessly as Gabe propelled them along. James and Gin just sat drinking in everything. Gabe allowed them a few minutes of leisure to absorb the scene and to watch him and learn as he paddled the boat without scraping the side and making lots of noise. "You guys think this is a pleasure cruise or something? Grab a paddle and let's get going. That includes you too, Captain, I mean, sir." James laughed but then picked up his paddle and began paddling.

They learned all kind of fishing techniques that day. Ways that had been passed down from generation to generation of fishermen. They learned how to fish for bream and how to hook a white perch in the top lip so that he wouldn't get away. Gabe was a treasure of fishing knowledge, and he shared it all with them.

Gin didn't mind baiting her hook too much, but she wasn't excited at all about taking her fish off the line. Gabe told James to take them off for her.

"Now just a minute," said James. "I'm the captain here, right? She should be taking fish off for me, not me for her."

"Let me teach you something about leadership, son. If you truly want to be a good leader, you have to become something else first."

"What's that?" asked James.

"First you have to be a servant," said Gabe.

"A servant! You've got to be pulling my leg."

"There's nothing greater that a person can do than to give up his life for a friend. It doesn't always mean actually losing your life, although in some cases it may. You can also give up your life by putting others ahead of yourself. Being a servant means helping and doing for others. Any great leader, whether a soldier, politician, minister, or even a mom or dad, must serve others. In turn, they will be considered the greatest leaders by those that they serve."

James thought about it for a minute. "I think I understand," he said.

It was getting dark by the time they loaded up and left. As Gabe refastened the cable, frogs had begun a melodious concert welcoming the new night. There were the little tree frogs as well as other types of frogs all around. The deepest bass and loudest were the big bullfrogs. James and Gin sat quietly drinking in the night sounds. The sights and sounds of the day had been a feast within themselves. Somewhere nearby, a whippoorwill crooned its lonely cry, and way off in the distance its mate returned the call. It was calling him home.

For just a few moments, Gabe sat quietly, transported in his mind to his new home that he knew was soon to come. He thought of Naomi and how he missed her. In his mind he could hear her voice again, calling for him to also come home. For Gabe, death was not an enemy, not a fate to be dreaded. Although he was in no hurry to go, Gabe knew he had nothing to fear. Death was not an unknown to him, it was not just darkness, it was not an end, it was a door. Not an ordinary door, but a door that would open one day and that he would pass happily through to an eternity of joy, love, and happiness. The whippoorwill's lonesome cry resounded once more snapping Gabe back to the present.

Gabe told Gin and James that he could not recall when he'd had so much fun fishing. "I believe it's the best trip I've ever been on, and you two made the difference." Little did Gabe know that that day when he laid his fishing pole down, he'd laid it down for the last time.

CHAPTER XXI

J ames was awakened the next morning by his dad. "Time to get up, tiger, 'gonna' do things a little different today."

"What's that, dad?" James asked as he stretched and yawned.

"What we need is a little routine around here," said his dad.

"Oh no," thought James, "another program for the family."

"Yep, starting today we are going to get back to normal around here. First, we are going to have a big family breakfast, and then we are all going to church."

"Aw, dad, come on. It's 6:30 in the morning. I'm tired."

"Doesn't matter, get up, bathe, and get dressed because we're going out."

"All right, all right, I'm up." Pretty soon the whole house was a bustle of activity.

By 10:55 the whole family was sitting on their old pew at church. It had been so long since they had been to church. All the hymns and good times they had missed came back in a flood of memories. Everyone told James how glad they were that he was back. When he actually thought about it, it did feel pretty good to be back. Some people did stare, but he had gotten used to it by now and just didn't pay it any mind.

When the preacher started his sermon, he said he felt led to change his sermon topic for such a special occasion as this. "Today," he said, "We will take another look at 'The Good Samaritan.'"

For thirty minutes he preached about helping our brother and how we all have someone who is willing to stoop down and lift us up even when we do not deserve it. Then, as he closed his sermon James heard his name mentioned. "Yes," he said, it has been about six-months since James and his family were in that tragic accident. But by some miracle, James is still here with us today. James could have died from his injuries. He could have lost his whole family. But by a miracle, they are all here today. One part of that miracle was a man. A man that God used to save James. No one ever found out who that man was. The police say they know but were sworn to secrecy. This man found James when no one else could. This man was his 'Good Samaritan.' We may never know who that man was. And maybe it's better that we don't know. For some time, America has grown cold toward helping others. Isn't it comforting, knowing that there is someone out there who cares? It may be your husband. It may be someone's dad or grandad. But isn't it wonderful to know that he cares? Jesus is someone else who cares. He's out there in that forest, He's out on that highway, He's down the street, and He's in this place today and He cares for you. He loved you so much that he took your sins upon himself and died in your place. Take your hymnals as we close---."

James had very little memory of that night. Yet this reliving of the accident brought back memories, foggy and faded, but memories just the same. He was very quiet the rest of the day. Inside a great struggle was taking place. He wanted to know; he had to know! That night he had trouble sleeping; all night long he tossed and turned. It wasn't because his dad said that he had to go to school the next morning. It was because of the haunting memory that had been awakened by the preacher. All night he heard the sounds of screams of terror, and glass breaking and metal twisting and bending and---.

"James, come on, son. It's time to wake up, time for school." Although James was a little scared, he was also a little excited to be back, to get on with his life. What he regretted most was that he knew that Gabe would be there to finish up the job that morning, and he would miss it. As he was getting ready to leave, Gabe was coming in.

"Good 'mornin,' old partner," said Gabe.

"Mornin," said James.

"Off to school I see."

"Yes sir, it's back to the old grind."

"Well, be tough, you can take it. Show 'em' what you're made of."

"Yes sir," James said as he saluted.

"It'll be alright, son, just you wait and see."

Smiling, James slowly made his way down the new ramp holding onto the wheels of his chair in order to control the rate of his decent. As he reached the bottom he stopped and froze for a moment in deep thought. Something Gabe had said sounded familiar. James turned back around but saw only an empty doorway. The muffled sound of Gabe laying out his tools for the day brought peace to his mind and he could picture Gabe meticulously and carefully laying his tools out on a mat or towel. Slowly, hesitantly, James began to move forward.

The morning went pretty well for James. His teachers were understandably apprehensive about having him back in class. They had heard talk around town about how he had changed since the accident. They didn't know how he'd act back in a classroom with all the pressures. They also didn't know how the other children would deal with the situation.

When James arrived at his hall, there was a large banner hanging overhead that said, "Welcome Back, James- We Missed You." Many of the students stopped and stared, mostly just out of curiosity. James, however, knew exactly what was going on. He decided it was time to give them a little taste of their own medicine. But he wouldn't be mean like he used to. He would find a better way to do it. He could feel their eyes on him, following him as he rolled down the hallway. He decided to see whether he could catch them off guard.

When he felt sure that someone was staring at him, he would suddenly stop and spin the chair around and say, "Thanks, I'm fine and how are you?" Most of them were so shocked they were either speechless or mumbled in an unintelligible language, something akin to Martian.

Each of James' teachers were very considerate but did not pamper him. They took into account his needs but made him work just as hard as the rest of the students. Each teacher asked whether he would like to take ten or fifteen minutes to share his experience with the class. James was more than eager to share. He opened each talk the same way.

"My name is James Whitman and I may be handicapped to a certain degree but I am not a cripple. I may be in a wheelchair, but I can still fish, work on things with tools, play ball, and do almost anything I used to do before the accident."

He took a few minutes and told how the accident happened and all the treatments and therapy he had to go through. He also told what caused the accident, how someone out to have fun took something from him that he could never give back.

"So, don't feel sorry for me because I'm not a cripple. Actually, there are many things that I have improved on since the accident. I guess even though it was bad, some good has come out of it. There are all kinds of races that we run in life. Some are on the track, and some are in the classroom. Others are at home, while still others may be somewhere on a job. Just remember that when you're running the races in your life and you hear a noise behind you, don't bother turning around because it will be me fixing to pass you."

All the different classes clapped when he finished. His homeroom gave him a standing ovation. By the end of the day word had spread throughout the school. The principal, other teachers, and even the secretaries had dropped in to hear James. All of his friends patted him on the back and were really excited to have him back at school, except one.

James was finishing his last, little talk and all his classmates were applauding except Chip. Chip sat in the back of the room seething. He was the man about campus. Everyone liked him, but today he was being totally ignored. In two different classes he had been fed this garbage about wheel-chairs and not being a quitter, and he was full of it. And he was full of "Mr. Goody-Two-Shoes," too. He'd fix him. Yep, he'd fix him good.

Gin had been having a very different kind of morning. Down the halls and in class Gin noticed that people had begun to stare at her. All morning people turned and whispered as she approached them. Several times she had picked up on conversations. She had heard incriminating words escape the little private parties going on in the hallways and classrooms. Two of the words were "wheel-chair" and "cripple." She didn't know about all the good things that had been happening.

Now she was humiliated and embarrassed all over again. There was nowhere to hide; no dark hallways to duck down or shadows to fade into. She wished James and she didn't have to go to the same school. She knew that she would be labeled, "The girl with the cripple," for life. She wished that she could crawl under a rock and never come out.

After lunch, classes on second lunch shift had a twenty-minute break. Gin stuck her head outside the hall door and scanned the surroundings. There was no sign of James, so she stepped out into the bright sunshine. She found an isolated bench and sat down alone.

How was she going to deal with all this? How could she live like this the rest of her life? The cool air and warm sunshine felt good to her. It reminded her of the day they went fishing. "That was a good day," she thought to herself. Everybody was so happy and she even caught six fish.

She was suddenly jolted into reality by angry words coming from a nearby crowd. She looked but couldn't tell what was going on. "It was a large mob of about twenty," she thought. "It must be a fight." Her theory about fights was to try to be anywhere else possible when one happened. The last thing she needed was to have to call home from the office because she had been involved in a fight.

As she turned to leave, a twinkle from the crowd caught her eye. "What was that?" she thought. It almost looked like a camera flash it was so bright. Then it flashed again. The she realized that the sight was the sun reflecting off of something. The crowd shifted momentarily, and this time she saw the bright sun glint from the chrome wheels of a wheelchair.

Chip had waited all day for this moment. He had plotted, planned, and connived every spare moment, building his hatred until the fuse was almost burned away down to the dynamite. He watched James as he left the building with a new friend pushing him in his wheelchair. It seemed that the big thing on campus to do today was to push James around. "Yes, sir, I'm fixing to do some pushing myself," thought Chip.

Although James was quite capable of getting around on his own, everyone else wanted to push him around. Since it seemed to give them such pleasure, he just went ahead and let them do it. He didn't really have any particular place to go; he just let them push him all around the campus.

Chip saw him headed east down the sidewalk. Quickly he circled the lunchroom and mentally plotted an intercept course with James. If he paced himself just right, he should meet them where the sidewalks crossed. Chip slowed down and then realized they were walking faster than he thought. He picked up the pace a little but maintained it too long and was about to get there ahead of them. He could feel and actually hear the "thump, thump, thump," of his heartbeat in his ears.

Chip momentarily paused as he approached the crossing, then stepped directly in front of James. The chair caught him on the leg, and he stumbled and fell to the ground. It was quite obvious to everyone who was at fault. Chip was not the adept actor that he presumed himself to be. Chip grabbed his leg and stumbled to his feet.

"Are you ok?" James asked.

"You stupid invalid! Why don't you watch where you're going? Are you blind too? Can't you see me, or is it just that you are brain damaged too?"

"James did not say a word. Inside he was a boiling cauldron, but he forced himself to remain calm. His silence and self-control served only to make Chip more and more angry. Suddenly the crowd around them started to part. Gin was pulling people out of the way to get to the inside of the crowd. In Gin's imagination, James was a helpless little boy again with peanut butter and jelly all over his face and hands. Gin found Chip and put her finger right in his face. No longer was she worried about making the call home from the office. Now it was about blood, about family, about her family.

"Hey you!" thundered Gin. Chip turned and gave her his full attention. He wanted attention but when he turned, he wasn't expecting to face the storm that was brewing in the face of James' sister. Getting in his face and pointing a finger, almost touching his nose, Gin asserted herself.

"Hey, James is my brother! If you're going to try and start a fight with him, you're going to have to go through me first!"

Gin fell silent and slowly lowered her hand as James raised his hand toward her indicating that she should stop; that she should back off. Gin's face was still blood red to attest to the tales of redheads and their tempers. Slowly Gin backed away.

Now it was Chip's turn and he was getting ready to fire with both barrels.

Returning his glare toward James, "Who do you think you are anyway?" asked Chip. "You think you are some kind of a hero or something! Why, if you were so smart, you wouldn't even be in that chair!" James continued to sit quietly and listen. He only looked straight at Chip, looking sympathetically right into his eyes. "What are you looking at?" yelled Chip. "Why are you looking at me that way?" he continued pumping his fingers open and closed repeatedly making a fist.

James continued to just sit quietly and listen. He looked as if his feathers were not even ruffled.

Chip struggling to regain a foothold continued, "The newspaper said you didn't even wear a seatbelt, and we all know that's just plain stupid."

James still continued sitting quietly allowing Chip to slip and slide on thin ice of his own making. While at the same time, Chip was slipping closer and closer to a hole that he couldn't dig himself out of. James allowed about five seconds to pass before he said anything. What he did next was one of the hardest things he had ever done. The crowd anxiously waited on him to say something smart back to Chip or to try to hit him. A mob mentality was rising to the surface of the stewing hullabaloo. Several of the students who admired James stood ready to pounce on Chip. They stood with clinched jaws and were leaning forward toward Chip. They were only waiting on the word JUMP from James. The tension was so high one could almost taste it. James chose his words carefully and spoke them calmly.

"You're right," said James. Whatever word Chip was about to say froze in his throat and he was left speechless with his mouth gaping open. James continued, "If I had worn my seatbelt, I probably would not be in this chair, but then again, I guess we'll never know. I can guarantee you I'll wear my seatbelt from now on. I really wish the accident hadn't happened. But I can't stop living either. You see, the accident happened on my birthday, some birthday present, huh? Do you remember what you got for your thirteenth birthday Chip?"

"Uh, yeah, I got a bike, I think."

"Well, I got this chair, not my idea of a four-wheeler. I bet you wouldn't be willing to trade, though, would you?"

"No, no, I guess not," stammered Chip.

"Chip, I really do care about you and all my other friends. That's why I made those little speeches today. To be honest, when my teacher asked me about doing this, I was terribly scared. I didn't make those little speeches today because I think I'm somebody important or because I'm smart. I gave those talks hoping that everyone will listen and not wind up like me or cause someone else to. You see Chip, I really do care and I care about you too!"

As Chip was about to speak, he was rescued by the bell ringing to return to class. By now the fire had disappeared from his eyes and he actually looked pale. To think, he had actually tried to provoke a fight with someone in a wheelchair. The floodgates opened and reason began to return flooding his brain and emotions with calm and worse, shame. How could he have been so stupid? How could he have let his temper blind him so?

James decided to break the ice first, "Hey, buddy, Chip," James called. Chip snapped back to reality out of his deep thought. "You know, you have to stoop pretty low to fight somebody in a wheelchair don't you Chip?"

Chip hung his head in shame and appeared disoriented. Thunderstruck, he had no words to give in response. He knew he was wrong, so wrong in all that he had thought and done or attempted to do.

"Yep, you'd have to stoop pretty low to do that Chip. Probably even have to get on your knees, huh?" James said chuckling.

Everybody laughed as the tension subsided and the mob began to fragment as students began to break away and drift back to class.

Chip also chuckled nervously as he was thinking the same thing about having to stoop so low.

"Let's go, buddy. Time for class. How about giving me a push?"

"Sure," said Chip. Then off they headed back toward the building.

Gin kind of stumbled off in disbelief. What did she just witness? James had found another way to stand on his own two feet. Maybe James was going to be all right after all.

CHAPTER XXII

After school, Gabe came back over. "Well, this will almost finish us up," Gabe said. "I put on a coat of varnish this morning. I'm going to put on another coat this afternoon. Tomorrow we'll finish the last step."

"So, what is the last step?" James quizzed.

"Oh James, you won't believe what we're going to do to this patch tomorrow."

"Come on, give me a hint," persisted James.

"No, no that's my secret. Tomorrow my friend, you will know. Unless, of course, you can figure it out on your own," Gabe winked.

James and Gin both watched as Gabe cleaned the dust away and carefully applied the last coat of varnish. Cautiously Gabe brushed the varnish in the direction of the grain that he had surgically placed in and on the patch. He only lifted the brush at the end of the stroke as he tapered off the varnish onto the original finish.

Stepping back, Gabe explained how important it is to brush in the same direction as the wood grain. It helps to enhance the look and to help it blend in.

"Now, it's very important that you not let anyone step on or even near the patch until tomorrow."

"You can count on us," proclaimed James. He raised his arm and pointed his finger into the air and with a deep manly voice pronounced, "The King's treasure shall not be disturbed! And now, the King's night shall retire to the throne room. I'll be back in a minute," he said in a sheepish voice trying to be funny.

Gin rolled her eyes, "Brothers," she said.

"But aren't you glad you have one? Even if brothers can be silly and embarrassing sometimes."

"You mean all of the time," said Gin.

"Mr. Michaels, sir."

"My, what formality," said Gabe. He stopped what he was doing and turned to face Gin.

"I just wanted to thank you for all that you have done for James, actually for all you've done for us, for all of us. You can't imagine what it was like trying to live with James before you came. I really had grown to hate him. You should have seen him today at school though. You would have been so proud of him. Even though he was in a wheelchair, he was able to stand on his own. He took care of himself and did it in a way that most adults wouldn't or couldn't have been able to handle. He told all his classes that he wasn't a cripple, that he was whole again. That he could do almost anything he wanted to and some things even better. He also told them how the doctors patched him up, but it took a carpenter to heal his wounds, to build him back up. He said his wounds were deep, the deep kind that doctors cannot even see. He was afraid, he thought his wounds would kill him even months after the accident because they were deep enough to destroy him from the inside. He didn't know what to do, where to turn and then one day someone showed up. That someone made a difference. That someone was you Mr. Michaels."

Gabe turned away from Gin, pretending to be putting away his tools, but Gin had already seen the moisture in his eyes and the way he had to swallow hard.

"You really didn't hate him Gin. You may have hated the way he acted but you really didn't hate him. We can still love people even when they aren't lovable. Sometimes that's when they need our love the most. Believe it or not the Bible actually talks about that very thing. Romans 5:8 says that while we were yet sinners, Christ died for us. God loves you Gin and I love you and James too."

Gin threw her arms around Gabe's neck and hugged him like she would never see him again.

The new front door began to open, and Jim and Fran stepped in.

"Watch your step," Gin exclaimed.

"Hey, that looks great!" said Jim. "It really does. I'll be glad to pay you right now, Mr. Michaels. Will a check be all right?"

" 'Naw,' you just don't worry about that right now. I'll run back by tomorrow. I have one more, little thing to do to the patch to make it look really natural; you know like the rest of the floor."

James came rolling back down the hall listening to every word that was being said.

"Really," Jim said. I would like to go ahead and pay you. I trust you and know that you are a man of your word. If you say you'll be here I know you will do everything in your power to do so."

"Looks pretty good doesn't it?" asked James.

"Almost natural," said his mom.

Gabe was gathering the last of his tools when Jim returned with a check.

"See you tomorrow Mr. Michaels," Jim said. Gabe shook his hand and told him goodbye.

"Thanks again, Mr. Michaels," said Gin.

Gabe winked at her. "Anytime honey," he said.

Everyone left the room and went about his business, except James.

"Gabe are you all right?" he asked. "You look a little pale, and your hands are trembling."

"Oh, I'll be ok," said Gabe. "I'm just like that old truck out there, we're both getting old and shaky. Now you don't be 'worrin' about me, James."

Gabe squatted and looked right into his eyes.

"You're a fine young man with a great future. Don't ever lose your faith. You don't have to go to the moon to do great things. Most of the time, the great things people do go totally unnoticed. There are great rivers to cross and mountains to climb everyday in our lives. As you swim those rivers and climb those mountains, give others a boost to help them over, and you'll become a great man."

Gabe finished packing all his tools and cleaning up. James followed him out the door as he headed for his truck.

"I'll come back tomorrow after school and finish the floor. I really do think you'll be surprised what I'm going to do to that patch. Especially since we worked so hard to make it shiny and pretty."

The old engine sputtered and then roared to life. Carefully, Gabe started backing out of the driveway. When he backed into the road, he turned again, and their eyes met one, last time. Gabe threw up an old, rough, calloused hand and waved goodbye. James waved in return. As he pulled away, James saw the old, faded logo on the side of the truck again, "Gabe's rolling fix-it shop. If you can break it, I can fix it."

"You sure can," thought James. For some reason unknown to him, James waved one last time and then yelled out, "I love you, Gabe."

The old truck was down the street now, but James could still see Gabe's silvery hair in the back window. James sat there until the roar of the old engine faded away and the sound of a bird singing took its place. He listened to the beautiful melody for a moment imagining that Gabe would have done exactly the same thing. James rolled his chair back inside then slowly closed the door to the outside, symbolically dropping the curtain on this stage in his life.

Kenny was a bright six-year old boy with a big imagination. His creativity, as his mother called it, had gotten him into trouble on more than one occasion. Many a sleepless night had been spent by his teachers trying to figure out how to redirect his energies into a more positive direction.

Today, Kenny was a motorcycle policeman. Yesterday, he was a bank robber. His mother thought there was, at least, some hope. At least today he was on the right side of the law. She didn't even suspect that for tomorrow he was planning to be a fire chief. Already he had a pack of matches hidden in his dresser drawer and had started collecting firewood out back.

Kenny sat behind the bushes at the top of the hill. "Yes sir," he thought. "The next car that comes by here speeding is getting a ticket."

About the same time, he heard the loud roar of an old engine coming up the other side of the hill.

The old, green pick-up crested the hill. When Kenny saw it, he almost laughed. He wasn't about to chase an old man in an old raggedy truck like that. The old man gave him a big wave as he passed. Kenny waved back just as a reflex. "I wonder how he saw me?" he thought.

Gabe saw the little, freckle faced, red-headed boy long before he got to the bushes where he was lying in wait. Kenny's bright, red hair betrayed him in the evergreen bushes like a sore thumb. Kenny let the old pokey truck pass as another car, a red sports car, conquered the top of the hill.

"You're mine," Kenny said. In a flash, Kenny was on the sidewalk and racing down the hill. His motor, a piece of cardboard he had on his spokes, purred rhythmically as he sped faster and faster. The car was beautiful. It raced by the old green pick up as if it were standing still.

"Look at him go," mouthed the junior motorcycle policeman. He began to mouth a siren wail, and his feet pedaled faster and faster.

DAVID PERKINS

Kenny didn't even notice the end of the sidewalk racing toward him as he gained speed. When he finally did turn to look, he saw to his surprise, that he was headed right into another street. By then it was too late to do anything. As he hit the end of the sidewalk, he became airborne and flew off the curb. The bike landed with a sickening crunch and flipped over and over dragging Kenny along with it. They finally came to a stop right in the middle of the busy highway. Gabe was already pulling the truck over against the curb as the front wheel on the bicycle screeched to a stop.

Kenny's left foot was pushed through the spokes of the rear tire, and the tire itself was bent and twisted around, pinning his leg. He lay crying loudly, calling for his mama. Gabe had stopped on the other side of the intersection and was running toward Kenny at full speed. Gabe first heard, and then saw the tractor trailer as it charged over the top of the hill.

Gabe was exhausted and breathless from running. Through his tears, Kenny saw the mammoth truck about the same time Gabe did. Like a wild animal he started thrashing and clawing at the ground, screaming uncontrollably while trying to get out of the way of the truck. By the time Gabe reached him, Kenny's world was the roar of the diesel throttling down, the grinding of the brakes, and the rubber of the tires being burned away by the asphalt as it thundered toward him.

Never looking up, Gabe grabbed Kenny's leg, spun the wheel back around and ripped his foot free of the spokes. Kenny scrambled away just as the truck made contact.

For many years Kenny had nightmares about that day. Over and over he relived the sights, the sounds, and the smells of that moment. But the vision that haunted him the most was the kind blue eyes that he saw for only a split second. They were branded into his memory forever. "Who was he?" Later, he found that he was just an ordinary carpenter who was willing to give up his own life so that a rambunctious, rebellious little boy could live.

CHAPTER XXIII

The next afternoon James waited patiently for the old truck and the old man that never appeared. Five times he had gone outside listening for the rumble of the old engine and returned each time more and more despondent.

"Why would he lie to me?" he asked at the supper table.

"Well, James, what makes you think that he lied?" responded his dad.

"He could be sick, or something more urgent could have come up," Gin chimed in.

"But he's always done what he said he'd do. It just isn't like him to leave a job unfinished. Especially when he is within a few minutes of being finished."

Although James was disappointed that Gabe hadn't shown up, he was much more disappointed thinking that Gabe may have lied. His brain began running down all kinds of dark alleys. In his heart James knew something had to be wrong. Perhaps Gabe really didn't care about him as much as he had said after all. The least he could have done was to call. Deep down inside though, James knew that Gabe would never break his word without a good reason. But where was he?

Growing more and more downhearted, James finally resigned himself to the fact that Gabe may never return. James spent most of the night tossing and turning in his bed. Sometime before daybreak his tired mind finally surrendered and he got an hour or two of sleep.

The day after was more of the same. There was still no sign of, message, or call from Gabe. Then things changed.

The next day Fran went to pick up James and Gin at school. On the way home, Gin was showing James some sketches she had done in art class. Gin looked up as the car began to slow for no apparent reason. Fran eased the car off the side of the road and rolled to a stop. James was too busy critiquing Gin's sketches to bother looking up.

"Hey mom, what's going on?" James questioned as he flipped to the next sketch.

"Nothing sweetheart, just a funeral."

"But why did you pull over?" mumbled James as he continued flipping pages in the art pad, still not bothering to look up.

"It's what we do in the south, it's called respect, respect for the deceased and compassion for their family. It won't take long."

But it did. The line of cars seemed to go on forever. The entire procession had their lights on and it almost reminded them of military precision. Each vehicle was slowly passing by; each one, equally spaced from the other. James, Gin, and Fran thought it was somewhat unusual that there were so many cars from all over the country. There were license plates of every color and description.

"I've never seen anything like this in my life," said Fran.

For a full seven minutes the cars slowly rolled past. Gin and James had unbuckled and turned around as much as possible to see how many out of state license plates they could count. Fran had already cranked the car and was getting ready to pull back out onto the road as the end of the long line of cars approached. James and Gin were already buckling their seatbelts when James suddenly froze.

He was the first to hear it. The sound was muffled because their car windows were raised. But there was no doubt about that sound.

Sure enough, the old green truck was the last in line. James could see a black bow tied on the handle of the truck. He strained to see Gabe. He stretched, cupping his hands around his eyes searching for the grey hair and the blue eyes that he knew would be behind the wheel. The back of the truck was over-flowing with flowers, along with two vans of flowers in front of the truck.

"That's why he couldn't come!" exclaimed Gin. "He had a death in the family or a close friend or something."

Because the bright sun was in their eyes, none of them ever got a really good look at the driver. James, though, said he was sure that he saw the driver's gray hair. "But," James thought. "It just wasn't the same. Somehow it looked different."

Fran pulled slowly onto the road, and James followed the old pickup with his eyes as it slowly descended over the hill behind them. James stared without blinking so long his eyes started watering, but he was almost sure he saw his friend raise a hand and wave in the small, back window of the old truck.

The rest of the afternoon James waited and listened for the engine of the old truck. But Gabe never arrived.

Late that afternoon, Jim came in from work, looking like he'd lost his very best friend. As he walked through the back door, he neglected to give Fran the customary hug and peck on the cheek. He just looked at her and said, "Where's James?"

"In the living room I think, why?"

Jim turned and walked out of the room without saying a word.

James was sitting in the living room, which by now was almost dark. He had been sitting there ever since they had gotten in from school. Homework was not even considered, and everything else was completely forgotten. Only one thing haunted his thoughts, a gray-haired, old man with blue eyes.

No one bothered to turn on the lights even though the sun had set. As Jim entered the room, James heard the footsteps but didn't bother to even look up. He knew his dad's gate, his stride, and the sound his shoes made on the floor. Turning his head slightly, to his dad's left he saw a bright, shiny spot on the floor. Realizing that it was Gabe's and his patch made his head wilt once again.

Placing his hand lovingly upon James' shoulder his dad squeezed it ever so slightly as if James were a baby again. James turned his face up to look at his dad and the dried tears appeared as squiggly rivers on an old map; indeed, James had aged and matured over the last few weeks.

In his hand, Jim held the local weekly paper. Delicately, he laid the paper across James' lap as if the paper were a new born infant.

"I'm sorry, James," he said. Then he turned and walked out of the room.

James' hands were shaking as he reached down and picked up the paper. Slowly he opened it and held it close. In the shadows it was difficult to read. In bold print the headlines read, "LOCAL CELEBRITY LOSES HIS LIFE SAVING YOUNG BOY."

James' eyes followed the headlines down to the print. "His life ended as he had always lived it. Kenny Brown son of Bill and Kathy Brown, was snatched from the jaws of death by Gabe Michaels---." James didn't read on, he couldn't see anymore.

The rest of the week passed by slowly. They read the article and found the cemetery where Gabe had been buried. The obituary had listed him as a World War II veteran, a father, a grandfather, a deacon, a Sunday School teacher, a carpenter, but mostly, a friend to all.

They went to the cemetery and were amazed. The grave looked more like a garden center than a grave site. There were flowers everywhere even though the family had requested that in lieu of flowers to please make donations to Veterans Organizations or to The American Cancer Society. Gabe was so beloved that people did both. The flowers even overlapped over onto other lots even though the family had already donated all the potted plants to local nursing homes and shut in senior citizens. Most of the flowers were from local citizens and family. However, there were some from rather unusual senders.

There was one large wreath from a group called, "The Good Samaritans."

Jim scratched his head, "Must be one of those gospel groups or something."

There was also another wreath from a group called, "Gideon's Knights." Across the wreath was a banner which proclaimed, "Serving the many with only a few."

Another one was sent from a group called, "The New Disciples."

The most unusual piece was one in the shape of Noah's ark. It had a banner which said, "Save the Animals." The card said the wreath was from the old gang of, "The Ark Club."

James sat in his chair very still while staring at and scanning the scene, absorbing the landscape of flowers. Softly, he mumbled something unintelligible. Jim looked to Fran and Gin but they were also clueless as to what James said.

"What's that James, what did you say?" asked Jim.

He's still here. Just look all around. Gabe is still here. He left part of himself here, in all these people, in Gin and you, and mom, and me. He gave a little piece of himself to all of us that knew him. He will always be with us as long as we live and maybe if were lucky, we can pass a little of him on to others and even on to our children.

The ride home was very quiet, hardly a word was spoken. Every one of them still in a sense of shock, all still trying to process the events of the past few days. When they got home, Fran asked Gin for some help with the laundry. Normally, Gin would have groaned and complained but for some reason today, she jumped right in and went to work. When Gin moved the dirty clothes hamper, she noticed something in the corner behind it. Reaching in, she let her fingers search for the lost clothing. The article turned out to be the pants that she had worn fishing. Somehow, she had managed to overthrow the basket that evening.

She began the tedious job of checking all the pockets. In the right front pocket, she felt something rectangular. The pants still smelled of fish, and she was extra cautious how she handled them. Suspending them with only two fingers on her left hand she gently reached into the pocket with her right hand and to her surprise found the note that Gabe had given to her that day. The same note that he had given to her in case anything happened to him.

Emotions poured into her like a flood over a waterfall. Gin's knees buckled and she collapsed, sitting down right on top of the pile of dirty laundry. One moment she was weak in her stomach, the next she was elated and excited at the thought that Gabe was there in the room with her again, reaching out to her through the note. What was in it that he wanted to tell her?

"James come here, quick!" Gin yelled. Regaining the strength in her legs, Gin stood and ran to where she thought James was and they met in the hallway.

"What is it? You act like you've seen a ghost!"

"It's Gabe," she said acting as giddy as a little school girl.

"What do you mean it's Gabe?"

"You remember the day we went fishing?"

James' eyes froze momentarily staring off at a scene back at the lake and an involuntary smile grew on his face for just a moment. Returning to reality, James said, "Yeah, so. I remember, it was just a few days ago."

"Do you remember when Gabe gave me the note?"

"Yeah, I guess, so, why?"

"He wanted me to keep it, but he never asked for It back."

Gin turned her fist over and slowly opened her fingers. Laying in her palm was a small blue piece of paper that had been folded several times into a neat, crisp edged, blue rectangle.

For a few moments they just stared at the note not knowing whether to open it or not. They both felt funny about reading it. It was almost as if Gabe were speaking to them from the grave. Slowly Gin began to unfold the note. James didn't try to stop her. They both knew it was something they would eventually have to do. Gin began to read.

Dear Gin and James,

If you're reading this note, it probably means that something has happened to me. I have a serious medical condition that could and will ultimately lead to my death, short of a miracle. If I should suddenly get very ill or if I should collapse and still be alive, Gin, you will have to drive the truck for help. Find the nearest house with a telephone and have them call for help. I hope it's nothing worse than just being a little sick. Use good judgement no matter what happens. Don't do anything foolish like driving too fast for help. Nothing that happens to me is your or James' fault. I'm ready and I know where I'm going when the end comes. Besides, I've got people waiting there wondering where I am and why I'm not there already. If this is my day, I'm just glad that I got to spend my last day with you and James. I wouldn't have wanted it any other way. Now remember, don't panic. Everything will be all right, just wait and see. It will be all right, I promise. I love you both.

Gabe

PS: James, finish the patch.

James looked up at Gin. "I don't know what to do! Gabe said to finish the patch, and I don't know how. He said I would be surprised at what he was going to do to it after we had worked so hard to make it perfect. But he didn't tell me what to do!"

James solemnly rolled back into the den and stared at the spot. It looked finished. It was beautiful.

James tossed and tumbled in bed again for hours but sleep would just not come. Sleep eluded him all night. In his head he could hear Gabe saying, "What are you doing in bed when you haven't finished the patch?"

About six o'clock, Jim heard a crash outside. Startled, he sat straight up in bed. "What in the world was that?" Jim blurted. Looking out the window Jim could see that it was still dark outside.

"The noise sounded like it came from the utility room," said Fran. "I put some more canned pears out there yesterday. You don't think—"

"Yes, that's exactly what I think," said Jim. "I told you those shelves were not strong enough to hold any more weight." Turning over Jim said, "Go back to sleep. The damage is already done. We can clean it up later this morning."

James lay on the cool, damp ground somewhat shaken but unhurt trying to figure out what to do. Going down had been a breeze, but getting back up the ramp had proven too difficult of a challenge. Fighting against the frosty ramp and gravity had all but whipped him. On his fifth attempt at the summit, the right wheel of his chair had slipped off the edge of the icy ramp and catapulted him out into the front yard.

About five o'clock in the morning, James had gotten out of bed and gone back into the den. Something was bothering him. There was something about the patch that just wasn't right. He looked at it from all angles. He looked at it from the right. He rolled around and looked at it from the left, then high and low. He was baffled. It looked perfect to him. It was beautiful.

Shaking his head in frustration, he rolled himself into the kitchen and made some hot chocolate. Meticulously he cleaned and straightened up the kitchen behind himself as he had recently learned to do. He rolled himself to the table and began sipping on the warm, rich cocoa.

He leaned back in his chair and stared into the living room. "Gabe, you didn't tell me what to do," he sighed aloud.

He sat and stared a long time, scanning the entire living room floor. He could see the silhouette of himself sitting in his chair as it cast a shadow across the beautiful oak floor. "It's ok," he said to himself as he stared at his counterfeit image. One day, I'll walk again. I'm ready for the world, and it had better be ready for me!"

Looking beyond his shadow James could see the patch glistening from the kitchen light. "There's nothing else that can be done to it. How can you improve on per-fec------tion?" His voice trailed off to a whisper.

"That's it! That's it," he said aloud as loud as he dared. "Gabe promised when we finished the floor that you wouldn't be able to find the patch."

"That's what it is; it's too perfect. The patch was practically shimmering in the middle of the floor. The rest of the floor doesn't match. How could I have been so blind?"

"I know what Gabe would say," he thought. "People can be blind or handicapped in many different ways. People can be blind even when they can see."

"Look at it, it sticks out like a sore thumb," said James. "We know what to do about that now, don't we?"

James had been on the ground for a long time, how long he didn't know. Finally, he reached down and checked his pocket to make sure his precious sandpaper was still there. He had worked too hard to retrieve it from the utility room to lose it now. He was sweating profusely from all of his efforts to get the chair back up the ramp. He knew he couldn't stay there in the dark and on the cold, icy ground until morning. But he had to rest, if only for a moment.

As he lay there in the early dawn twilight, he began to think. It was almost as if this were a dream. James felt like he had done all this before. All alone in the dark, the night sounds, it was all too familiar. Visions from the accident began to flash before his eyes. He remembered the accident, the squeal of the tires, the grinding and twisting metal, the rolling car, and the shattering class.

Then he remembered something else. In his mind he could see blue eyes glowing in the light of a flashlight. He could see silver hair, an angel maybe or----------.

James gathered strength from somewhere down deep inside and began pulling himself across the crunching, icy grass toward the ramp. The ramp was like a mountain to him, but bravely he conquered the summit that stood in his way.

Gin was awakened by a scraping noise. Her first thought was that it was a mouse. Frightened, she awoke her mom and dad. Together they tip toed down the hall to the living room. The front door was wide open and the cool morning air was flooding into the living room. James was lying on the floor beside the patch. Carefully and methodically he was wet sanding the patch with fine sandpaper. James looked up, his eyes were puffy and red. Tears rolled down his cheeks and fell from his chin onto the newly dulled patch. The patch, now blended in, made the floor look as good as new.

"I remember," he said as he wept, "I remember."

His dad walked over and ran his fingers through James' ruffled, grass-filled hair.

"It'll be all right, son, just you wait and see; it'll be all right."

The familiar words warmed James as he thought about the first time he'd heard them so long ago down beside a rippling stream deep in the forest.

Just one old man. Just a carpenter, was all he was. But he was one. When one adds to one then there are two. When love, compassion, care, and knowledge are shared, the effect becomes exponential and lives are touched and changed all over the world. As Gabe passed from the earth that week, it made a difference. For years he would live on in the hearts of the people who would live after him and tell the story of the old carpenter with the big heart.

However, there was now one more apprentice waiting in the way to take his place. One old soldier faded away, and now a new one had come, full of life and ready for service, a soldier of life.

The wide-open doorway behind James framed the old, majestic maple which stood like a sentinel in the front yard. Sunbeams from the birth of a new day were already illuminating its form and bringing it into focus. A gentle breeze began to stir the one, beautiful, golden leaf remaining on the old maple.

The leaf began to quiver with excitement as the breeze became more intense. Finally, tired of fighting, it relented to the wind's gentle urges. Breaking away, the leaf momentarily flipped end-over-end and out of control. But then, sailing with the wind; it developed its own glide pattern and gently twirled ever so slowly and gracefully and settled to the ground. In the place where the leaf had broken away, barely visible, was the tiny, green tip of a fresh spring bud.

Message from the author:

I hope you have enjoyed reading **_SPLINTERED_**. This book was written for the express purpose of helping others. I do pray that it has been a help to you in some way. I appreciate your input and comments and will read each and every one. Thank you for taking your time to read **_SPLINTERED_** and for any comments you may choose to leave.

Made in the USA
Columbia, SC
11 August 2020